THE INVINCIBLES
TEAM TWO
BOOK FIVE

RIPPED

USA TODAY BESTSELLING AUTHOR

HEATHER SLADE

RIPPED

© 2022 Heather Slade

Paperback:
979-8-88649-143-2

ripped
/ript/
verb
tear or pull (something) quickly or forcibly
away from something or someone
adjective
having high muscle definition

MORE FROM AUTHOR HEATHER SLADE

BUTLER RANCH
Kade's Worth
Brodie's Promise
Maddox's Truce
Naughton's Secret
Mercer's Vow
Kade's Return
Butler Ranch Christmas

WICKED WINEMAKERS
FIRST LABEL
Brix's Bid
Ridge's Release
Press' Passion
Zin's Sins
Tryst's Temptation

WICKED WINEMAKERS
SECOND LABEL
Beau's Beloved
Coming Soon:
Cru's Crush
Bones' Bliss
Snapper's Seduction
Kick's Kiss

ROARING FORK RANCH
Coming Soon:
Roaring Fork Wrangler
Roaring Fork Roughstock
Roaring Fork Rockstar
Roaring Fork Rooker
Roaring Fork Bridger

THE ROYAL AGENTS
OF MI6
Make Me Shiver
Drive Me Wilder
Feel My Pinch
Chase My Shadow
Find My Angel

K19 SECURITY
SOLUTIONS TEAM ONE
Razor's Edge
Gunner's Redemption
Mistletoe's Magic
Mantis' Desire
Dutch's Salvation

K19 SECURITY
SOLUTIONS TEAM TWO
Striker's Choice
Monk's Fire
Halo's Oath
Tackle's Honor
Onyx's Awakening

K19 SHADOW OPERATIONS
TEAM ONE
Code Name: Ranger
Code Name: Diesel
Code Name: Wasp
Code Name: Cowboy
Code Name: Mayhem

K19 ALLIED INTELLIGENCE
TEAM ONE
Code Name: Ares
Code Name: Cayman
Code Name: Poseidon
Code Name: Zeppelin
Code Name: Magnet

K19 ALLIED INTELLIGENCE
TEAM TWO
Coming Soon:
Code Name: Puck
Code Name: Michelangelo
Code Name: Typhon
Code Name: Hornet
Code Name: Reaper

PROTECTORS
UNDERCOVER
Undercover Agent
Undercover Emissary
Coming Soon:
Undercover Savior
Undercover Infidel
Undercover Assassin

THE INVINCIBLES
TEAM ONE
Decked
Edged
Grinded
Riled
Smoked

THE INVINCIBLES
TEAM TWO
Bucked
Irished
Sainted
Hammered
Ripped

THE UNSTOPPABLES
TEAM ONE
Furied
Merried

COWBOYS OF
CRESTED BUTTE
A Cowboy Falls
A Cowboy's Dance
A Cowboy's Kiss
A Cowboy Stays
A Cowboy Wins

Table of Contents

1

Rip

The last thing I expected when Vex requested a meeting was that he wouldn't come alone. When I saw a woman I didn't recognize in the front passenger seat of his SUV, I was even more baffled.

"Who is that?" I asked when I got out of my truck and met him in between where we'd both parked on the bottom floor of the underground parking structure.

"A complication." He looked over his shoulder as if to make sure she hadn't gotten out of the vehicle. "Her name is Pearl Fischer."

"Any relation to—"

He responded before I'd even finished the question. "Yeah, according to her, John Fischer was her father."

Fischer and his accomplice, both members of the Aryan Brotherhood of Texas—the ABT—had been shot and killed a year ago after kidnapping a woman the people Vex and I worked for were hired to rescue.

Then as now, Vex was undercover on a CIA-backed mission to infiltrate both the ABT and their parent organization, the Aryan Nation. His role, and mine, was focused primarily on the Texas chapter, while there was another team undercover at the national level.

"Why is she with you?" I asked. And why the fuck was I here? But he would get to that—I hoped sooner rather than later.

"As you know, the ABT has essentially split into two factions. Fischer was on the side that supports an ABT more in-line with the Nation."

Okay, so this *wasn't* going to be quick. "Your mandate."

"Exactly. I'm supposed to be 'cleaning up' the Texas chapter, particularly the assholes in the splinter group."

I chuckled silently. The Aryan Nation was a prison gang made up of street thugs, which meant their definition of "cleaning up" was subject to interpretation.

Vex's official cover was that he'd been the former leader of the Nazi Freedom Riders. In his role, he'd facilitated its merging with the Aryan Nation. After the merger took place, he was given the rank of colonel, above the usual highest of major at any state chapter.

"You still haven't answered the question about why Fischer's daughter is with you."

"Scottie picked up on some chatter about Pearl we don't quite understand."

McKenna Walsh, code name Scottie, was an agent with the Department of Homeland Security, on loan to the CIA and working undercover as Vex's common-law wife.

"What was the chatter?"

"Seems the splinter group has it in for the young woman—"

"What does that mean?"

"I'm getting to that, Rip. What Scottie overheard suggests Pearl wasn't actually Fischer's biological daughter."

That explained why he'd started out saying "according to her," she was John Fischer's daughter. However, I was getting really impatient really fast. *"And?"*

"Scottie heard one of them say that now that Fischer is out of the picture, they can use her to get what they want from the Aryan Nation."

Now that he was out of the picture? He'd been dead for over a year. "What do they want?"

"No idea, but evidently, she's valuable to someone in Idaho."

"Are you following up with the Nation?"

"Got my contacts inside seeing what they can find, but so far, neither John Fischer nor Pearl is on anyone's radar as being significant. I'm headed to their head-quarters now to see what I can figure out myself."

While this wasn't making much sense, Vex did start out by saying he and Scottie didn't understand the chatter she'd heard. "So, what? The 'splinters' planned to kidnap her? Ask for some kind of ransom?"

"Initially, at least. Scottie said they planned to have their 'fun' with her first."

"First?"

"Before they kill her."

"So you transported her off the compound? Risky."

"The cover is that 'Ms. Shay' and I have been called back to Idaho for a council meeting and took Pearl with us."

"Where is Scottie?"

"She had to rendezvous with DHS, so I took her by the safe house to get her car. We're meeting up at Austin-Bergstrom in about an hour."

"If the splinters believe this Pearl is of value, how would they feel about you delivering her right into the hands of whoever they think wants her?"

"I'm hoping it stirs them up."

"You got anybody on the inside of this group?"

"Negative, but I'm workin' on it."

"All right. Keep me informed." I took another look over at the SUV.

"Who does this woman think I am?" I asked.

"I know you from the Nazi Freedom Riders."

"Someone who didn't come over when you did?"

"That's right. You left gang life, but you're someone I trust to keep her safe."

"Does she know her life is in danger?"

"Affirmative."

"What am I supposed to do with her?"

"For now, take her back with you to the safe house." Vex spoke as if he was in charge of this mission rather than the other way around. However, I *had* asked.

"If she isn't Fischer's kid and the splinters believe she's of some value to the Nation, who the hell is she?"

"Good fucking question."

"All right. Anything else I need to know tonight?"

Vex shook his head. "Negative."

"I'll contact Money in the morning and make him aware of this development—see how he wants us to proceed."

Kellen "Money" McTiernan was the current director of the CIA. McTiernan used the firm Vex and I worked for—the Invincible Intelligence and Security Group—for jobs that fell outside what he could make happen within the agency itself—like the infiltration of a national terrorist organization.

"Who is this woman's mother?"

"Says she never knew anything about her. She's lived on the compound as far back as she can remember."

If that was the case, it meant her existence, at least for the most part, was entirely "off the grid." She'd have no identification, no money, and no way to get any. The ABT would've provided everything—no different than any other cult.

"I gotta be on my way," Vex said, looking at his phone. "She has some of her things with her. Oh, and her bear."

"Her what?"

"You know, a stuffed bear."

As in taxidermy stuffed or teddy-bear stuffed? I guess I'd find out soon enough. "Hey, Vex, how old is she?"

He shrugged. "Maybe late twenties."

2

Pearl

I held my breath when Mr. Robinson returned to the SUV where I waited. Instead of getting in the driver's door, he came around and opened mine.

"Come on. I'll introduce you to Rip. He'll take you somewhere you'll be safe."

He stepped aside, and I got out.

"Okay?" he asked.

"Okay?"

"Going with Rip."

I didn't have a choice one way or the other, did I? "Yes, sir."

After being introduced, I was led to a vehicle that looked exactly like the one Mr. Robinson drove. I got in and hugged my stuffed teddy bear, Mojo, tight to my chest, willing myself not to cry.

No matter what happened next, it had to be better than what I imagined the ABT had planned for me after

Ms. Shay told me I was in danger and needed to leave the compound.

I looked out the window when the tears I tried to hold back fell.

"Listen," said the man in the seat beside me. He didn't continue until I wiped my tears and turned toward him. "You're safe. I'm not going to hurt you, nor will I allow anyone else to."

"Thank you," I whispered.

"You're welcome. I haven't had a chance to get dinner. Are you hungry?"

"No, sir."

"When was the last time you ate?"

"I had lunch, sir."

"My name is Rip. You can call me that or nothing at all, but you don't need to call me sir."

"Yes, sir…err…Mr. Rip."

"Just Rip."

I nodded, but doing what he asked wouldn't be easy for me to get used to. On the compound, the only way I was permitted to address an elder was as sir or ma'am or with an honorific, like I'd just used.

"What do you like to eat?"

Like? I ate what was served. Even when I'd been on kitchen duty, it wasn't up to me to decide what to prepare.

"Burgers okay?"

"Yes. Thank you."

A few minutes later, he pulled into what I knew was a restaurant, not that I'd ever been inside one. "I can wait here," I said when he parked.

"You need to eat, Pearl. Is it okay if I call you that?"

I was taught to respond no matter what I was called. "Of course, sir—err—Rip."

"Would you be more comfortable if we used the drive-through?"

"I'm really not hungry."

"You said you liked burgers, right?"

"Yes, sir, but—"

He held up his hand, started the engine, and pulled out of the parking space.

"What can I get you?" said a voice through an intercom.

"Two double cheeseburgers, two orders of fries, and two chocolate milkshakes, please."

"You got it, sugar. Anything else?"

He looked over at me.

"No, thank you."

"That'll be eighteen dollars and twenty-seven cents at the window, please."

"I…uh…don't have any money," I said when he drove forward.

He looked over at me and smiled. "Even if you did, I'd never let a lady pay for dinner."

He was quiet while we waited for our food. When the woman handed him a drink holder and a bag, he passed it all to me, then pulled back into the same parking spot he was in before.

"It'll taste a lot better hot than if we wait until we're at the ranch to eat," he explained, motioning to the bag. "Yours is in there," he said after taking one burger and a container of French fries out.

He unwrapped the burger, dumped the fries next to it, and stuck a straw in the shake he'd put in one of the vehicle's cupholders.

I did the same, took a bite after he had, and nearly groaned out loud at how good it tasted. No wonder people ate at restaurants. This wasn't just the best burger I'd ever eaten; it was the best food.

When I took a sip of the shake, I felt my eyes roll back in my head. And the fries? I'd never had anything like them.

"Doesn't look like you have much with you. We'll need to get you some more clothes and other things tomorrow."

"Yes, sir," I said before taking another bite of food. I realized my mistake a few seconds later, but the man didn't seem angry that I'd called him sir again.

As for getting clothes for me, he knew I didn't have any money. There was no point in repeating myself. Maybe he intended for me to get some kind of job or do work for him on the ranch in order to pay him back.

"Misty can probably help with some of it."

"Is she your woman?"

"No, she's Hammer's housekeeper. He owns the ranch where I live."

If there was already a person who cleaned, they wouldn't need me to do it. I was sure there were other jobs I could help with, though. I had plenty of experience working in the fields.

Driving through the gates of the ranch wasn't a lot different than entering the compound, except there weren't any armed guards for us to check in with.

"That's where Hammer and his wife, Maeve, live," said Rip, pointing to the biggest house I'd ever seen. It was all lit up and looked like something out of a fairy tale, except modern and not at all rustic like the buildings at the compound were.

"This is me," he said, pulling up to another house that was still grand, just not on the scale of the first he'd pointed out. And it was harder to see since there weren't any lights on.

"I haven't been living here too regularly," he said, shutting off the engine. "Wait there." He got out, came around, opened my door, and held out his hand. I took it.

It felt so powerful, even more than my father's. Everything about him seemed that way. Rather than being afraid, I felt safe. Something I hadn't realized was missing since the night the elders woke me to tell me my dad had been killed.

Since then, most everyone on the compound had left me alone to mourn. Even though I was a grown woman, I wasn't permitted to stay in the small cabin my dad and I had lived in before he passed. Women weren't allowed to have quarters to themselves. They either lived with the men who had claimed them or in the women's bunkhouse. Mr. Robinson and his wife, Ms. Shay, had taken me under their wing, though, and insisted I move in with them.

Since Mr. Robinson, a colonel from the Aryan Nation, outranked everyone else on the compound, they abided by his command. Even Major Nichols, who had been the senior elder up until the colonel arrived, followed his orders.

Tonight, though, everything in my life had turned upside down. I'd been back in my room for a couple of hours after finishing my kitchen duties when Ms. Shay knocked, then entered.

"Pearl," she'd said. "Mr. Robinson and I have learned you're in danger. He's taking you off the compound tonight. Now, in fact," she'd whispered. "Hurry and grab a few of your things. We need to leave."

Ms. Shay led me to Mr. Robinson's SUV, which was waiting in an area that couldn't be seen from the compound's main buildings. Before we got in, she hugged me. "We're taking you somewhere you'll be safe," she'd said. Mr. Robinson then drove to a house in the city and dropped her off, saying he'd meet up with her later.

Now, here I was, about to enter the home of a man I didn't know, out in a world I knew next to nothing about living in.

3

Rip

While Vex had suggested I take Pearl to the safe house where I'd been spending the majority of my time, I didn't agree. More importantly, I didn't answer to him. I was the lead on this mission. He was undercover and followed my orders.

Tomorrow morning, I'd check in with Money, brief him about her being with me, and see if he had different thoughts than mine about how best to handle this.

The Aryan Brotherhood of Texas wasn't just a cult. It was a prison gang made up of some of the nastiest fuckers to walk the planet.

Vex said the story they'd come up with was that Pearl would be accompanying Scottie and him to Idaho. He'd need to come up with another to explain why she didn't return to the compound when he did.

There would likely still be suspicions, but it was doubtful the splinter group would have reason to start looking for her right away.

Regardless, keeping her here on the ranch was the safest option. I'd need to make Hammer aware of her presence as soon as I could, meaning tonight. I also needed to alert Fury.

While she and I were nothing more than a booty call for each other, I'd been out of touch far more often than not in the past few months. If, by chance, she arrived here for a meeting with her boss—Hammer—and happened to notice I was home, she just might decide she had an itch I needed to scratch.

On the other hand, she'd made it clear she and I were not exclusive and she'd put up with no "typical cowboy bullshit" from me. Her exact words. Maybe since I'd been gone so much, she'd already found someone else to mess up sheets with.

"I'll show you how to use the alarm, and we'll program your code in the morning," I said as I punched in my own. There were other security protocols we followed on the ranch, but there was no point in getting into those tonight, either.

The house felt warmer than I'd expected it to, which likely meant Misty had already been here and turned up the heat. I punched a code on my phone that turned several lights on throughout the place.

Pearl gasped. "How did you do that?"

"Smart lights," I said, showing her the app on my phone. "This controls pretty near everything in the house."

"That turns on the lights?" She pointed at my phone. "Unbelievable," she added under her breath.

"This here will be where you'll stay," I said, leading her down the hallway and opening a door to a room I'd never used. It was furnished, though, like the rest of the house was.

I'd spent too much of my life traveling to the far reaches of the globe—to some of the world's worst hellholes. When Hammer had offered me the ranch manager job and explained he understood the work I did for the Invincibles came first, I jumped at the chance to finally have a place I called home.

While I didn't own the house or the land it was built on, I'd known Hammer a damned long time. When he told me the place was mine for as long as I wanted it, I knew I could trust that meant I could stay here until the day I took my last breath.

Pearl looked at me with wide eyes. "This is for me?"

"Yes, ma'am." I opened the door across the hall. "This is your bathroom, and before you ask, it's all yours too. My room is on the other side of the house. You'll have all the privacy you need."

"Thank you, sir."

I hoped Pearl would get used to calling me something other than sir, but it would take time. Me nagging her about it wouldn't make it happen any quicker.

"Who's that?" I asked, pointing to the bear she was practically choking the stuffing out of.

Her cheeks flushed deep red. "This is Mojo, and I know it's silly to have him, especially at my age, but…"

"Go on," I prompted. "Finish what you were going to say."

"He's the only thing I ever had that's all my own."

"I'll tell you what, Pearl. I understand that better than you might think." I motioned for her to follow when I went into the kitchen. I was pleasantly surprised to find Misty had stocked the fridge when I checked. That meant I was right to think she'd turned up the heat.

"Looks like Misty paid a visit," I said, hoping she left some cookies. I opened the cupboard, and sure enough, there were a couple dozen of my favorite—oatmeal chocolate-chip. I grabbed the bag, opened it, and held it out to Pearl.

"No, thank you. I'm still full from dinner."

I took two, zipped up the bag, and put it back where I'd gotten it. "If you change your mind and want a snack before you call it a night, you know where to find 'em."

"Maybe just one."

"Attagirl," I said, smiling as I took the bag back out and handed it to her. "Want a glass of milk to go along with it?" I poured one for her and one for myself when she said she would.

Pearl took a bite and studied the cookie. "This is good." The look on her face wasn't anything like the one she'd had after she took a sip of the milkshake.

"Not a fan of oatmeal chocolate-chip?"

"No, I am."

"But?"

"Nothing."

I pulled out a kitchen chair and motioned for her to take a seat. "Come on, now. Fess up. There's something you don't think is quite up to snuff."

Her cheeks flushed like they had earlier when I asked about her stuffed animal, which I'd just noticed she must've left in the bedroom.

Pearl leaned forward. "Could use more butter," she whispered as though there might be someone else in the house who could hear her.

I took another bite. "I think you're right."

"I can make some if you want."

"Yeah? You like to bake cookies?"

"Not just cookies."

"Tell me what else."

I listened as the woman seated at my kitchen table listed her favorite things to cook. Every so often, she'd stop talking, almost as if she was embarrassed to have prattled on for so long, but with a few words of encouragement from me, she'd start right back up again. The longer she went on, the more color came into her cheeks.

In some ways, she looked older than she had a few minutes ago, and in others younger. Vex said he thought she might be in her late twenties. That seemed about right to me. I wasn't much older—three or four years, maybe.

Her hair was dark red, not quite auburn, and her blue eyes were almost too big for her face. She was a looker, that was for certain. Maybe even one of the most beautiful women I'd ever seen, now that the worry that had etched her face slowly diminished.

On top of a plain white T-shirt, she had on a denim jacket that looked handmade, and the black pants she wore were threadbare. When she covered her mouth and yawned, I noticed the pale skin of her hands bore signs of hard work.

"Have you ever ridden a horse, Pearl?" I blurted, wishing I hadn't when her face fell.

"It wasn't permitted."

"Would you like to?"

Those big blue eyes peered up at me. "I would."

"Attagirl," I repeated, getting up to sneak one more cookie before I called it a night myself. "I'll take you to the barns in the morning."

Pearl squared her shoulders. "I can earn my keep. Whatever needs to be done, I can do. I'm a hard worker."

"That's good to know and another thing we can discuss in the morning. Speaking of which, we could both use a good night's rest."

"Yes, sir." She stood, picked up our glasses, and cleaned them in the sink before drying them off and returning them to the cupboard I'd taken them out of.

While part of me thought about telling her I could do it, or even that it could wait until morning, I sensed Pearl would feel more comfortable making herself useful.

Once I was sure she was settled, I opened HALE—an encryption protocol developed by one of the founding partners of the Invincibles for the firm's proprietary use. It was the most secure voice-and-messaging app in existence, far superior to what the general population or even the government used—except for Money, of course.

Via that protocol, I sent Hammer a message, asking him to respond when he could talk "privately."

He called almost immediately.

"There's been a development," I began.

"Got a call from Vex earlier."

I nearly growled. It was one thing for him to make suggestions as to how I handled certain things on the mission. It was another entirely to go above my head and speak to *my* boss, not his. And even then, I didn't report to Hammer in my role with the Invincibles. He was my boss at the ranch.

"You still there?" he asked.

"Yes, sir. So, anyway, you know I have John Fischer's daughter with me."

"Roger that. I'm also aware you returned to the ranch tonight."

"If you'd prefer she not be on the property, I understand. It was a spur-of the-moment decision, and—"

"Stop right there. This is your mission, Rip. You make the decisions, and you don't answer to me about them. As far as her being on the ranch, if you believe she's safer here—which I agree—then this is where she should be. This place is battened down tighter than a ship's hatches in a storm."

"Thanks, Hammer."

"You got it, and just so you know, I gave Vex a dressing down for contacting me directly. It wasn't his place."

"Appreciate it."

"One other thing."

"What's that?" I asked.

"Never mind. None of my business."

"No, go ahead. I want to hear whatever it is."

"Fury's been asking about you."

"My next call."

"Glad to hear it."

While I knew Fury was a night owl, it was still late, so instead of calling, I sent a text from my personal messenger rather than through HALE, asking her to get in touch. When I didn't hear back right away, I wasn't sure if I was relieved or worried. However, if she decided to pay me a visit, I would know the minute she arrived at the ranch gate.

Before I got myself ready for bed, I walked over to the other side of the house. Since it was quiet and the lights were off, I figured Pearl was asleep or at least didn't need anything.

For the next hour, I lay awake, thinking about her. After accepting the fact I wasn't going to get sleep anytime soon, I got up and researched "cult survivors." While I wasn't sure putting those words into a search engine would yield the results I was looking for, there were pages and pages of information on the topic.

The recurring themes in every post or article I read focused on healing and recovery followed by empowerment.

In the short time I spent talking to Pearl this evening, I'd witnessed glimpses of all three. She'd started out timid, subservient, afraid to speak. By the time we shared Misty's cookies, she was "empowered" enough to tell me she believed they needed more butter, as well as offering to make a batch.

For someone like Pearl, who hadn't joined the cult of her own volition and knew no other way of life, recovery would look very different than for someone who had decided to join and subsequently had the choice to leave.

The other recurring theme in everything I read focused on female subservience, whether it be sexual or otherwise. Pearl was an innocent. That was obvious. The subservience part, though, she had down in spades.

However, I saw just enough fire in her to believe that once she felt comfortable, felt safe, she would blossom, come alive, maybe even be willing to help us take down the ABT.

That trust had to be earned, and it had to go both ways. I needed to believe she was trustworthy, especially for now, given she thought I was someone from the Nazi Freedom Riders.

My mandates, as I saw them, were to allow her to heal and recover, find her own sense of empowerment, and eventually, see if she'd be a willing source of information. But was I the best person for that job? Would a female operative be better suited? My gut told me no. However, it was something I'd discuss with Money tomorrow.

I checked my phone one last time before setting my laptop aside. Since there was nothing from Fury or anyone else, I closed my eyes and hoped I'd be able to sleep.

When I woke, the sun was rising and there was a racket coming from my kitchen. I pulled on my jeans and went out to investigate.

"Good morning," I said when I saw Pearl, her back to me, mixing something in a bowl.

She dropped the spoon that had been in her hand and spun around.

"I'm sorry. I didn't mean to startle you."

Rather than answer, Pearl's gaze traveled the length of my body and back up again.

I realized my error in not putting on a shirt. "Be right back."

"I hope I didn't wake you," she said when I returned, this time properly dressed.

"I'm usually up by now. Did you sleep okay?"

I caught a glimpse of her smile. "It was quiet."

"Is that good or bad?"

"Honestly? It was divine."

"Yeah?"

"No snoring."

"I see."

"My daddy was quite the snorer."

I nodded. While I felt bad she'd lost her dad, if he was her biological father, I knew enough about the kind of man he was to believe she was better off. If he'd been a more honorable man, he would've gotten her away from the damned ABT.

"My nana was quite the snorer too. I can attest to that." I smiled, thinking about the woman I'd spent so much time with when I was a *youngen.*

"Who was that?"

"My mama's mother. She could make a mean batch of oatmeal chocolate-chip cookies. I think that's why they became my favorite."

"I bet she put more butter in them." Pearl lowered her voice when she said the words, which also made me smile.

"What are you making now?"

"Pancakes. With blueberries. If that's okay."

"Another favorite, and anything you want to cook, you are more than welcome to. How about some coffee?"

She set the spoon and bowl aside and wiped her hands on a dish towel. "Um, where do you keep the grounds? I didn't see any."

"I meant, would you like some coffee? I wasn't asking you to make it."

"Oh. Um. Yes, please."

I walked over to the one-cup machine and got two pods out of the drawer below it.

"Too bad your phone can't do that too," she said over her shoulder.

My phone, the moment she said the word, vibrated with a message from Fury, also not sent via HALE, asking what I was wearing, hoping it was nothing, and to send a photo. It was typical of the texts I received from her. I smiled, shook my head, and shoved the cell in my back pocket.

When I looked up, Pearl was studying me, but immediately dropped her gaze and went back to the pancakes.

"I'm heading to the barns after breakfast, if you'd like to come with me."

She set a plate in front of me. "Would you like syrup, sir?"

"No, thank you, *ma'am*. These look plenty good all on their own. So, the barn?" I said between mouthfuls of the best pancakes I'd ever had. When she didn't answer and I looked up, I noticed she wasn't eating. "Don't like pancakes?"

"I'm waiting until you're finished, sir."

I set my fork down, folded my hands in my lap, and kept my eyes on her. "No."

"No? What do you mean?"

"We'll eat together."

"I can wait."

I stood and picked up my plate. "That isn't how it's going to go in my house." I walked over to the trash bin.

"What are you doing?" she gasped.

"You don't eat, I don't eat." I kept my voice low and even.

"I was just waiting until you're finished."

"You eat with me. Not after me. And my name is Rip. Or Zane, if you prefer. Either one works, but sir doesn't." I still had my plate in my hand, not that I had any real intention of throwing the pancakes in the garbage. "Well? What's it gonna be?"

"Okay. All right. I'll eat with you."

I didn't move a muscle. "Get a plate, and sit your butt in a chair at that table. Just like you did last night."

"Yes…Rip."

I waited until she was seated before getting two more pancakes, then joining her.

"Here's another thing. My mama raised me that you answer—with words—if you're spoken to. Anything else is considered disrespectful. Particularly when someone asks you a question."

"Yes…Rip," she repeated.

I could tell it was damned hard for her not to say "sir," but she'd eventually have to learn not to. It was one thing to use honorifics when speaking to a commanding officer or, in Hammer's case, a boss. But at the kitchen table, it wasn't gonna fly.

"I'm waiting."

Pearl looked up at me with wide eyes. "What for?" Her voice was barely above a whisper.

"Do you want to go to the barns with me this morning?"

"I would, thank you."

"There. Isn't this better? We're having a nice conversation." I stood to get more coffee and was about to grab hers too since it was nearly empty. "Want another cup?"

"Yes…please."

"Yes…please…who?"

"Yes, please, Rip."

"Now we're gettin' somewhere."

4

Pearl

It shouldn't have been a surprise that Rip wanted me to eat at the same time he did. Last night, I hadn't hesitated. It was just when he read the message on his phone that I got flustered. I could tell by the look on his face it was from a woman. Whatever she'd said, made him smile. Then, rather than respond, he put the phone in his pocket.

While I'd never had a man of my own, I paid attention to how the couples on the compound flirted with each other. Or didn't, when the woman was claimed by a man who didn't treat her right.

Rip was obviously the flirting type, and in the short few hours I'd been here, he'd treated me better than any man ever had, besides my father and Mr. Robinson.

When he surprised me in the kitchen and I'd spun around to find him in nothing but his jeans, I was stunned almost speechless. He was the finest-looking man I'd ever seen, and that was with his clothes on. Without a shirt, he almost didn't look real. The muscles of his flat stomach were so well defined I could've run my finger over their ridges. The top button of his jeans was open too, so I could see a little of the hair that trailed downward.

Unlike most men at the compound, his body wasn't covered with tattoos. The ones he had were mostly on his left arm, which was completely inked. The only other one I saw was right above his heart. It read, "Survival of the Fiercest." I liked that.

I wanted to be fierce someday. It definitely wasn't something that would've happened while I lived on the compound. Although I suppose I'd always had a bit of ferocity deep inside me. I could remember my dad and me playing lions and tigers when I was little. I *loved* to growl, so I always wanted to be the lion. Or a bear, like Mojo.

I was a little disappointed when Rip had hurried off and came back a few minutes later wearing a shirt and boots. I'd liked seeing his bare feet. He was so handsome, with a strong jaw and thick, wavy, dark hair. He kept his beard neat and trimmed. I liked that too. The best thing about him, though, was how nice he was. He'd been that way since he first shook my hand.

He'd gotten cross with me a couple of times, but I hadn't felt scared or threatened. Every word he spoke was with respect. He joked around with me too. Another thing I liked a lot.

If this was what it would've been like on the compound if someone like Rip had wanted me, I wouldn't have minded at all. It was the fear that I'd end up with a mean man that had made me beg my daddy not to let it happen.

At first, he said it was because I was too young. Then he told the elders he needed me to stay and help him since he hadn't claimed a woman of his own.

I knew the other women on the compound thought I was "stuck up" or that I believed I was better than they were. At the time, I didn't care what they thought. As far as I was concerned, all the women were pretty much equal. Until Ms. Shay arrived with Mr. Robinson.

There was just something about her. The way she carried herself. From the minute I met Ms. Shay, I knew I wanted to be more like her. She was a little fierce. Maybe that's why I was drawn to her.

She wasn't stuck on the compound, either. She and Mr. Robinson left all the time and went places. Maybe they'd even come here sometimes to see Rip since he and the colonel were friends. I sure would like that.

"Did you bring clothes fittin' for the barn?" Rip asked as we cleaned up the breakfast dishes together. I'd offered to do it myself, but he insisted on helping. Actually, he said he'd do it since I cooked, but I didn't feel right about that, given it was his food.

"Is there something wrong with what I have on now?" I was wearing the same pants I had on last night but a different shirt. My boots were worn, like everything else I owned, but the soles were sound enough that I could work in the fields wearing them.

"Sure. That'll work. Later, we'll see about getting you some other clothes."

I had to look away when my eyes filled with tears. I'd known what I wore wasn't as nice as Ms. Shay's. All her stuff was store-bought, not handmade like mine were. Hers looked new too. There was nothing I could do about it, though. I sure couldn't ask someone to make me new clothes or get some from a store, either. Most of the time, it didn't matter. Now, I felt ashamed.

"Hey, Pearl, look at me."

I shook my head when more tears fell.

Rip walked around me and put his finger on my chin, forcing me to look up at him. "Do not feel embarrassed about your clothes or anything else. You made the best with the life you lived, and that is nothing to be ashamed of. I'm here to help you make the transition from living on the compound to living off it easier. That's all."

Living off it? What did that even mean? I'd never known anything else. I knew nothing about finding a place to live or getting a job. I'd never learned how to drive a car. I didn't even know how to ride a horse.

Rip dropped his hand, but his eyes remained on mine. "Tell me what you're thinking."

I shook my head and tried to step away, but he wouldn't budge.

"You don't understand. I don't know anything about your world."

"You're wrong. I do understand. That's why I said I'm here to help you. You heard that part, right?"

He smiled, and while I was feeling hopeless, I couldn't help but smile too.

"Pearl?"

"Yes…Rip."

"It won't just be me helping you, either."

"Who else?" Was he thinking about the woman he'd gotten a message from?

"I have friends who live here on the ranch, and they'll help. Misty, for one."

"Is that who the message was from earlier?" If it was, she might not be crazy about "helping" a woman who was living with her man.

Rip studied me. "You're a perceptive one."

"Is that a yes?"

"No, that wasn't Misty."

This time when I tried to move away, he stepped back so I could.

"Her name is Fury, and she's a friend. That's all."

When I walked out of the kitchen, he followed.

"You may think I'm stupid, but I'm not," I said. "I have plenty of experience with women who thought their man was looking at me a little longer than he should. They'd *never* say anything to him, but they found ways to get even with me for it."

"Like what?"

"Adding too much salt to the food I was preparing when my back was turned. Vinegar sometimes too, so the whole meal would be ruined and I'd be to blame."

"What would happen to you?"

I shook my head again. "Don't ask," I whispered, praying he wouldn't persist.

"I want you to tell me, Pearl."

"No." I went into the bedroom, but he followed me in there too.

"Tell me."

"I'd get a whippin'."

"With what?"

"A switch. Sometimes more."

Rip scrunched his eyes and took a step closer to me. "Hear this, Pearl. No one is going to be doing any whippin' here on this ranch, and especially in this house. And no woman is going to mess with you. No man either."

"Things are done when no one is looking."

"Fury isn't 'my woman.' Like I said, she's a friend. She's also a nice person." He sighed like my father used to sometimes. "Give yourself some grace, Pearl. The rest of us will too. Trust that."

"What is going to happen to me?" I whispered, unable to choke the words out otherwise.

"You're going to start over and create a new life for yourself in the same way so many of us have also had to do."

"I don't know how." I still couldn't speak above a whisper.

"You need help. Guess what? So do I. Wanna help each other?"

I smiled and nodded when he winked. "I like feeling useful."

"I really liked that you made breakfast. Most times, I leave the house in the morning without eating."

"I'm happy to do it. Anything else you can think of, too. I'd offer to clean, but I don't want to take Misty's job away."

"She only does it as a favor to me, so I'm sure she wouldn't mind at all. However, I don't want you to feel like you have to 'earn your keep.'"

"I like feeling useful," I repeated.

"That sounds good. Now, I have a few things to take care of, so we'll leave for the barns in about thirty minutes. Okay?"

"Yes…Rip."

5

Rip

I hoped, soon, Pearl would stop hesitating in order to remind herself how I wanted to be addressed. She'd made progress, though.

While I'd assured her Fury and I were just friends, I couldn't put off responding to her messages any longer, just in case she decided to come by the house and prove me wrong. It wasn't what I expected, but I'd learned with women—starting with my own mama—what you anticipated and what actually happened were sometimes two very different things.

I went out the back door and called rather than texted.

"Hey, Rip. Just the man whose pants I was hoping to get into later tonight. You back on the Hammered Dubliner?"

I chuckled. "I am, but I'm…not alone."

"Interesting. You've been keeping yourself busy while you were gone."

"Not exactly, but I do have a female houseguest who may be stayin' on quite a while."

"Even more interesting. Well, I'm a little disappointed for me, but I'm happy for you."

Maybe I should've explained further about Pearl, but then I might give Fury the impression that a nighttime visit would be welcome.

I also wasn't sure how many people I wanted to know she was here. I knew Fury was trustworthy. She'd joined Hammer's law firm and was an attorney for the Invincibles like he was. Before that, she'd been with the CIA, same as me. She'd been a damned fine agent but said she loved being an attorney more.

As far as others who worked on the ranch, there wasn't a single one who hadn't been thoroughly vetted. And by thoroughly, I meant as if each one worked directly for the CIA.

Every man and woman who earned a paycheck from the Hammered Dubliner knew the drill. Keep your head down and your mouth shut about what you might see or hear. That included Pearl stayin' with me and Maeve McTiernan livin' with Hammer before they were married.

Back then, she'd been charged with attempted murder. The judge on the case had agreed to an attorney's writ bond to let her out of jail while she waited to be tried. That meant she had to stay in Hammer's custody for the duration.

The charges were ultimately dismissed, but shortly after that, things took a different kind of turn when John Fischer—Pearl's maybe father—kidnapped Maeve. Since she was the CIA director's sister, the Invincibles were called in to rescue her. Fischer and another man had died the night it went down, and Vex's cover was almost blown.

Anyway, now Hammer and Maeve were happily married. Not just that; they co-owned my favorite bar—the Long Branch.

It wasn't too far from the ranch and had the best T-bones in all of Texas. The beer they poured was damned good too, and just about every night, they had live music.

Members of the ABT were banned for life from the place, but I still didn't think it was a good idea to take Pearl there and risk her being seen by someone we didn't realize was affiliated with them.

That would be true of anywhere she went, including into town to buy clothes. Maybe clothes were something we could order online. She looked to be about the same size as Maeve, but what the hell did I know about shit like that?

The other thing I needed to consider was that Maeve might not be all that happy the "daughter" of her kidnapper was living here on the ranch. Although, honestly, it would surprise me if she reacted in a negative way. That woman didn't seem to be intimidated by a damned thing in life, including being abducted.

At the time, the Invincibles didn't realize Fischer and his sidekick had delivered her straight to Vex, who was so deep undercover with the ABT and the Aryan Nation no one could get in touch with him. From what he'd later said, Maeve had stood up to him even when she thought he might kill her.

Before going inside, I gave Money a call. When I explained the chain of events that took place over the course of the last few hours, all he asked was that I keep him abreast of what else transpired. It was one of the things I liked best about working with the man. He saw no need to micromanage. On the other hand, he was at the helm of the most powerful intelligence agency in the world. He hardly had time to.

Next, I called my "other boss" a second time.

"Hey, Hammer. I need to talk to you about Pearl," I said when he answered.

"How's she doin' this mornin'?"

"She makes mighty good blueberry pancakes, I can tell you that much."

Hammer laughed. "Maeve's favorite."

"That's why I'm calling. Indirectly."

"What are you gettin' at, Rip?"

"Pearl needs clothes, boots, and probably a few other things. I'm worried about taking her out and risking her being seen. So then I got to thinking that, maybe, we could order some stuff for her online. That led me to wonder how Maeve might feel, knowing Fischer's daughter—not that we're sure she is—is here on the ranch."

"You've been doing a helluva lot of thinking for this early in the morning, my friend."

"No kidding. Oh, I wanted you to know I talked to Fury. It was easier to let her believe I had a woman I might be romantically involved with, staying with me rather than get into who she really was. I'm sure that will come up since Fury works with the Invincibles— that's one thing I didn't think about. Anyway, she and I are good. Said she's happy for me."

"I gotta admit, my head's startin' to hurt with all your thinkin'. Why don't I swing by later, and we can talk about this in person?"

"Roger that. Pearl and I are on our way to the barns now." I ended the call with Hammer after we'd agreed to meet up midafternoon. When I went inside, Pearl was waiting in the kitchen. Actually, she wasn't waiting; she was busy looking through the pantry and refrigerator.

"Whatcha' doin'?" I asked.

Like earlier, I startled her, and she put her hand on her chest. "I'm planning what to make for breakfast tomorrow. Dinner too, if that's okay."

"Breakfast, lunch, dinner. You cooking any of those will be absolutely okay with me. Cookies too," I added with a wink.

"To be honest, I haven't cooked for only two people since my father died. Even when he was alive, it wasn't that often. I'm trying to remember recipes for some things he liked."

"I want to talk to you about your dad."

Pearl set the bag of sugar she held down on the counter. "What?"

"Have a seat."

"Nothing good ever follows someone telling you to take a seat."

I smiled. "I wouldn't say this is going to be bad."

"Get on with it, then, please."

"What do you know about the night your father died?"

"He was shot."

"What else?"

"Nothing. It isn't the kind of thing the elders talk about."

"What about Mr. Robinson? Did he share any details?"

Pearl shook her head. "No, sir…err…Rip."

That surprised me, but Vex must've had a good reason not to tell her how her father died before now. Scottie must've too. However, it was time she knew the truth.

"Your father was shot and killed after he participated in a kidnapping."

I gave her a few seconds for that to sink in, although she didn't appear that surprised.

"Is that all?" she asked.

"No." I wanted to reach out and put my hand on hers, give her some kind of comfort, but I stopped myself. "The woman he kidnapped is Hammer's wife."

Pearl sat back in her chair, put her hands on her head, and it looked like she might be pulling her hair. This time, I did reach out, grabbed her wrists, brought her hands away from her hair, and held them.

"I'd ask if you're okay, but after hearing something like that, my guess is you're not. I know I wouldn't be."

Pearl looked at me. "Does she want me to leave?"

"She doesn't know you're here yet."

"I see. Does that mean you don't want me to go to the barns with you?"

"No. It means Hammer is going to stop by this afternoon and the three of us will talk about how best to handle this."

"Does he want me to leave?"

I squeezed her hands I still held. "No one wants you to leave. Okay?"

She nodded, but no part of me believed she didn't think I was lying to her.

"You are in danger, darlin'. Mr. Robinson and Ms. Shay told you that, right?"

"Yes, sir."

The sir thing came out when she was stressed or worried, that was becoming evident, and I wouldn't give her a hard time about it. "The problem is, they aren't sure from whom or why exactly. Do you have any idea?"

"I do not."

"We're doing our best to figure it out. That means, for now, the safest place for you to be is here on the ranch."

"Would it be okay if I didn't go to the barn with you?"

"First, tell me why you don't want to go."

It took her a while to answer, and when she did, what she said surprised me.

"I want to bake cookies."

"Now? Cookies can't wait until we get back?"

"Baking relaxes me."

I sat back in my chair and rubbed my stomach. "That will not be good for my waistline. However, I can't wait to get a taste of your recipe for oatmeal chocolate-chip."

"You don't have any chips."

"What?" I gasped. "Out of chips? I'm guessing you mean the chocolate variety."

She cocked her head. "Don't make fun of me."

I got up and grabbed a notepad and pen. "Write down everything you need for whatever you want to make. Or bake. Or both. I'll have Misty pick it up the next time she goes to the market."

She studied me for a long time before finally snatching the paper and pen and jotting several things down on it. I perused it when she handed it to me.

"Since you can't make cookies now anyway, why don't you come to the barn with me?"

"Are there chores you need me to do there?"

"Not really."

She pushed her chair back and stood. "I guess I can go with you."

"Attagirl."

6

Pearl

Baking really did relax me. Especially since I'd be in a small kitchen I wouldn't have to share with anyone. Or worry one of the other women was intentionally ruining my recipe.

You would think, given the way women were treated on the compound, they would've banded together rather than treat each other like the enemy. It wasn't everyone. It was more that certain groups of women liked each other but no one else. Then other women figured it out and did the same thing. And others. The only problem for me was I didn't fit in with any of them. There were one or two who had been kind to me—one really—but she kept her distance like everyone else. Her name was Ms. Opal. While she wasn't old, like some of the women on the compound, she remained unclaimed. I'd never asked why. Even if I had, I doubted she would've answered. Otherwise, I'd gotten on well with Ms. Shay since the day we met.

Maybe that was why the other women didn't like me—because Mr. Robinson and his wife took me in after my father died. *Was killed.* He didn't just die. He was shot after he'd kidnapped a woman.

I wasn't so naive to think he didn't do bad things. I knew most men in the ABT had served time in prison at some point in their lives. Some, many times. I also knew the way the ABT made most of their money was not legal. I suppose, like the other women on the compound, everyone assumed I'd look the other way. And I did, but I also paid attention. Especially when I went to live with Mr. Robinson.

It always seemed to me like he wanted to steer the membership away from crime, but since I wasn't privy—no women were—to what was discussed in meetings, I had no specific knowledge of it.

When those meetings were taking place, women were expected to do their chores, then read the Bible along with the teachings of the Church of Jesus Christ. I never paid much attention to what I was reading. Instead, I'd let my mind wander, not necessarily to anything in particular.

Rip motioned for me to follow him outside to where he'd parked last night.

"We aren't going to walk?" I asked.

"Mighty long walk from here, so no."

Also like he'd done last night, he opened my door and held out his hand to help me in. "Thank you, Rip."

He smiled. I guess until now, I hadn't realized how few men at the compound did that. Rip seemed to smile easily. Maybe it was his leaving the gang life, like Mr. Robinson had said. He sure had a nice house and must have a good job to afford it. Plus, it was nearly ten in the morning, and as far as I could tell, no one was looking for him to find out why he wasn't at work.

"What do you do for a job?" I asked.

"I'm the ranch manager here at the Hammered Dubliner."

It seemed like an odd name. Not that I knew what ranches were usually called. "What does a ranch manager do?"

"Mainly gets reports from the lead hands. Occasionally solves problems when they creep up. Certain times of the year are busier than others."

"When?"

"Spring and fall calving and branding are the busiest. That, along with when the herd needs to be medicated. Getting the bulls on the cows takes some work too."

I felt my cheeks flush. I knew exactly what that meant. I knew what all of it meant, actually, even though the cow-calf operation on the compound didn't seem to work out very well. Probably because none of the men running it knew what they were doing.

"You're inquisitive, Pearl. I like that."

"Feels good to be able to ask questions and have someone answer them."

"There they are," he said, pointing off into the distance.

"What?"

"The barns. The main ones anyway. There are some smaller outbuildings left over from when this was three different ranches. When Hammer bought them, what you see there became the primary operation center."

"He must know a lot about cows."

Rip laughed. "He knows next to nothing about them."

"So, why…? Never mind. Not my business."

"You can ask any question you want. If I can't give you an answer for one reason or another, I'll say so. As far as that question is concerned, my guess is you were going to ask why he bought three ranches if he knew nothing about cattle."

"Yes."

"Land. Wide-open spaces. That's what called to Hammer. He's an attorney by trade. In the beginning, he wasn't here much. Had to travel all over the world. Now that he's married, he's home a lot more. Plus, he and Maeve own a bar not far from here. It's called the Long Branch."

"Wow."

"That's why he hired me. To keep an eye on things when he can't."

"Last night, you said you haven't been living here too regularly." This was the first I'd seen him act like he wished I hadn't asked a question. Not that this was a question.

"I had some other business to attend to for the last few months. I still received regular reports from my team and was here when needed."

"Sorry. I'm being nosy."

"Inquisitive, and as I said, I like it, Pearl."

"What can I do?" I asked once we arrived at the barns and he showed me around.

"You and I are going to go for a ride." Another man came out of an office. He looked much older than Rip.

"This is Pete. Pete, meet Pearl."

Pete stepped forward, took off his hat, and stretched out his hand. "It's a pleasure to meet you, ma'am," he said. "My mama's name was Pearl. It's always been one of my favorites."

"Pete, Pearl here has never learned to properly ride a horse. We're gonna start working on that today."

"Should I get Daisy saddled up?"

"That's exactly who I was thinking. Why don't you give Pearl her first lesson in the workings of the tack room while I take care of a few things in the office?"

"Yes, sir. Come with me, ma'am."

"My name is Pearl. You don't have to call me ma'am."

When I looked at Rip, he winked.

"Have fun, and I'll join you as quick as I can."

While I'd never ridden a horse, I was plenty familiar with mucking out stalls, something Pete told me I didn't need to worry about when I offered to do it.

"This here is Miss Daisy. She's seen better days, but there isn't a sweeter, gentler horse on the ranch. You and her will get along just fine until you're ready for one with more spunk."

Pete showed me how to brush Miss Daisy, clean her hooves, and "saddle her up," as he'd called it. I never knew it was so complicated.

"We have plenty of hands willing to do this for you when you want to ride, but Rip likes doin' it himself. Says he gets to connect with his horse a little better before he takes 'em out to work."

"I can do my own too," I said, even though I didn't know the right words to use.

"Yep, I figured as much." Pete led Miss Daisy out of the barn and over to a hitching post, where he tied her off.

I cringed, looking everywhere but at the thing—not wanting to remember what had happened one night on the compound. I put my hand on my stomach, hoping I wouldn't get sick.

"You okay?" Pete asked.

"Um, yeah."

"What's goin' on?" asked Rip, walking up behind us.

"I don't want to speak out of turn, but I think something spooked our Pearl," Pete told him.

Rip turned to me. "What happened?"

"Nothing. I'm fine."

"Excuse us," Rip said to Pete before taking my hand and leading me into the barn. "I'm going to ask you again, and I want you to tell me the truth. Something you saw spooked you, like Pete said. Was it something or someone?"

"Something," I admitted, knowing he was only trying to protect me.

He looked out to where we'd left Pete with Miss Daisy. I didn't. "Jesus Christ," he muttered before calling out, "Hey, Pete, bring Daisy and Bart around to the other side of the barn. Grab the mounting block on your way."

"You got it, boss."

"Come this way." Rip didn't let go of my hand even after we walked out of the other side of the barn. "We'll talk about this later."

"Yes...Rip."

"None of that, now. We're gonna take a nice slow ride out a little ways. Pete and I will help you throw a leg over and find your seat in the saddle first. Okay?"

"Okay."

"This is a mounting block," Pete explained when he set what looked a lot like a step stool near the horse.

"I got Miss Daisy. Now, you throw a leg over, just like Rip said."

"Watch me." Rip put his foot in the stirrup and pulled himself up.

It took me a minute, but using the block made it easier. I doubted I could've gotten on like he had.

I listened and did as Rip and Pete told me to get Miss Daisy to walk, stop, and turn.

"Nothing fancy today. No fence jumpin' or anything like that," Rip said when we were a little ways from the barn.

We'd been riding for a few minutes when he brought Bart to a halt. I did like he and Pete had said and gripped the reins while I tightened my knees and thighs against the saddle. I had a feeling Miss Daisy would've stopped even if I hadn't, just because Rip's horse had.

"Think you can dismount on your own?" he asked.

"Let me see you do it first." I watched, then closed my eyes, going through his motions in my head.

"I'm right here. You aren't gonna fall."

I was more worried about kicking him than falling, but somehow, I got my leg swung over, and before I knew it, my feet were on the ground.

Rip walked both horses over to a fence and tied them off.

"Why did we stop here?" I asked.

"I wanna talk about what happened earlier."

"It was nothing—"

"I can't keep you safe if you aren't honest with me. It was the hitching post, wasn't it? Is that where they meted out punishment?"

I nodded, unable to speak. How had he known?

He put his hands on my shoulders and looked into my eyes. "You're safe here. Nothing like that is ever going to happen to you again."

How could he say that with such certainty? What if I was forced to go back to the compound? Surely, the punishment would be far worse then.

"Walk over here with me." When we got a little farther away from the horses, Rip lifted me and set me on the top rail of the fence before hoisting himself up beside me.

"See that?"

I looked where he pointed at the rolling hills that seemed to go on forever. "Is there something specific I'm supposed to see?"

Rip shook his head. "Nope. Just take it in. The wide-open spaces, the fresh air. Not another person around. You know what I call it?"

I shook my head.

"Freedom, Pearl. You're free, and you're never goin' back to the kind of life you led on the compound again."

7

Rip

Before we got back to my place, Hammer called, saying Maeve wasn't feeling too well, so he wanted to postpone our chat until tomorrow if we could. I was sure Pearl wouldn't mind delaying it indefinitely. Plus, it would give her and me the chance to get better acquainted.

One day turned into three, then five before Hammer called and said he was taking Maeve to see a doctor. When I asked if she was okay, he said she would be soon enough.

Pearl and I spent most days like the first one. After breakfast, we'd take a short ride out. In the afternoon, I'd tend to ranch business while Pearl either cooked a meal or cleaned.

Yesterday, I'd called Misty to talk about getting Pearl some more clothes and a better pair of boots. "She's about Maeve's size," I said when she asked.

Today, after our ride, I got a message from Misty, saying she'd left a few things on the bed in the guest room. When Pearl came out wearing a smile on her face along with something I hadn't seen her in before, I figured Misty got it right.

"How about the boots?" I asked.

"They're the nicest pair I've ever had," she said, looking down at her feet.

"I'm more worried about whether they fit."

"Perfectly."

I made myself a note to have Pete put a little something extra from me in Misty's next pay envelope and make sure I got the receipt for whatever money she may have spent.

Since it was also five days since I'd heard anything from Vex, I sent him a message via HALE early this morning, asking him to check in. While he had a mandate for his part of the op, I did too, and that was to make sure I knew where he was and what he was doing in the event Money asked for an update or we needed to brief him on something.

I received a response while Pearl and I were on our morning ride. However, I waited until we were back at the house to call him. Like I usually did when I made a call, I went out the back door. And as usual, Pearl kept herself busy inside.

"There's nothing," Vex said after telling me he and Scottie were preparing to return from Idaho. "John Fischer was a low-level ex-con no one paid attention to. Since the ABT operates somewhat autonomously—at least they have in the past—I couldn't find anything on the guy."

"What about Poltz?" He was the other man killed the night of Maeve's rescue.

"Nada."

"Obviously, nothing on Pearl either."

"Nothing immediately obvious. I didn't want to be poking around too much, given the ABT splinter group thought she'd be of value to the Nation."

The question that continued rolling around in my head was about Scottie overhearing the group say *now* that Fischer was out of the picture, they could use her to get what they wanted from the national organization. Why now? That part made no sense. They could've put their plan into action right after Fischer's death—or at any time in the past year.

"Were you able to get anyone inside the splinter group?"

"Affirmative. Shredder. He hasn't been able to find out why this asshole thinks the Nation wants Pearl, but he's working on it."

"Keep me posted, and good choice." Jeb White had worked the McTiernan kidnapping op, and even then, I wondered if I'd recognize him if I ran into him somewhere. Some people were like that. Nondescript, in a way that they were chameleonlike. And in this case, the guy's last name certainly fit.

"How are you going to explain why Pearl isn't with you when you return to the compound?"

"Those are the kind of questions that don't get asked—or answered—in the ABT or in the Nation, Rip."

Not that he could see me, but I shook my head. "That doesn't mean your splinter group isn't going to be curious."

"Maybe so, but the last thing they're going to do is show their hand by asking."

"You don't think they'll start poking around?"

"I did my own poking. Shredder was able to give me the name of the guy who was all fired up about using Pearl to get something from the Nation. It's Luke Howell, and he's made quite a few enemies with the council."

"What for?"

"Running his mouth and asking about things he shouldn't be. Every one of the guys in both gangs has something to hide. Most of them have enough that it would land them in prison for life if the wrong people found out about it. That or dead."

"What else is happening up in Idaho?" I asked.

"The infighting is escalating quickly. A new group has emerged who appears to be planning a coup of the current leadership."

"That's good news for us."

"According to Shredder, there were also power plays at the ABT while I was gone."

"Either faction making headway?"

"These assholes—both sides—couldn't fight an army of toddlers."

I got what Vex was saying. While every so often a "criminal mastermind" emerged from groups like the Nation, most of those in a gang like the ABT had never graduated high school.

As I'd said, power plays within either group were exactly what we were hoping for. It was the main reason both the Texas chapter and the Aryan Nation were on the verge of collapse.

Currently, and for the last almost thirty years, the national organization was led by a council of three—Kevin Edwards, Timothy Miller, and Christopher Pezak. The men had risen through the ranks when they were doing time in San Quentin. The Northern California prison was believed to be where the white-supremacist gang was originally formed.

Their power grab of the Nation had been rife with violence when they undermined then-leader John Clinton and took control.

Now, Clinton was serving consecutive life sentences in Colorado at the prison referred to as "Supermax." Some said he was set up by the current leadership, but every one of them, Clinton included, had committed a plethora of crimes they'd never be convicted for.

"Where does Bryan Nichols' 'loyalty' lie?" I asked.

Like Vex, Nichols had been undercover since shortly after the first raid the Invincibles were a part of. The

FBI sent him in when it appeared the ABT hadn't died the death they—and we—hoped they had.

"His cover is that he's none too happy the Nation sent me into Texas since, prior to my arrival, he, as major, was the senior elder. However, his 'stated' position is that he's very much aligned with the council. He's keeping a close watch on the splinter group."

"Do you think they're in cahoots with the ones planning the coup at the national level?"

"Makes sense. However, it still doesn't explain why they believe Pearl is of value to anyone in Idaho."

"Anything else I need to know right now?"

"I'll find out more once I'm back at the compound."

"Copy that. Watch your back. Scottie's too."

"Hey, Rip, how's Pearl doing?"

"Better than I expected."

"Even before the threat Scottie overheard, we were both optimistic that once we ended the ABT for good, Pearl would rally and find her way in the world outside the compound."

"I agree. She's got a fire in her belly. Smart too."

"Do you think she'd be willing to give up anything on them, or would her loyalties lie with Fischer?"

"I don't think she harbors any loyalty to the ABT at all. From the sound of it, she was already an outcast among the women, maybe even before her father—or whoever he was to her—died."

"Scottie and I did our best…"

"I know you did, Vex."

After ending the call with him, I sent Hammer a message asking how Maeve was doing. He responded almost immediately that she was a lot better after seeing the doctor and that he could meet this afternoon if we were available. I messaged back that we were, and he said he'd head to my place now.

When I went inside, I found Pearl in the kitchen, cleaning.

"Hammer is on his way here."

Pearl nodded but didn't look over at me. "Okay," she added after a few seconds.

"There's nothing for you to worry about."

"If you say so."

I took a step closer. "Pearl?"

"What?"

Before I could say anything else, I heard a knock at the front door. "That was quick. I'll let him in."

"Should I wait here?"

"Come out to the living room. We'll be more comfortable in there."

I opened the door, and he strode inside, introducing himself before I had the chance to.

"Sterling Anderson, but everybody calls me Hammer," he said, holding out his hand.

"Pearl Fischer," she said, shaking it.

"It's nice to meet you, and welcome to the Hammered Dubliner." Hammer smiled. "Damn, I like that name."

"It's unusual," Pearl murmured. "How did you come up with it? I mean, the Hammer part is obvious."

"My wife is from Dublin."

Pearl's cheeks flamed when he winked at her.

"Have a seat," I said, motioning to the couch and two chairs.

"I was thinking we should head straight up to the house. Give Pearl a chance to meet Maeve."

"You sure now is the best time? Is she feeling up to it?"

"Best to get it over with," Hammer responded.

"You okay with this, Pearl?" I asked.

Her eyes met mine. "It's only fair she knows I'm here." She looked at Hammer and raised her chin. "And it isn't right to ask you to continue keeping it a secret."

Hammer smiled. "Maeve is going to love you."

"Pardon?" she asked.

"You heard me." Hammer motioned for us to follow him out the front door. "See ya up there."

"What did he mean?" Pearl asked once we were in my SUV.

"Exactly what he said."

"How would he know if his wife will like me?"

"Maybe because you remind him of her."

Pearl shook her head and looked out the side window. "That makes no sense," I heard her mumble.

Hammer was already inside when we arrived, so we walked up to the front door and I knocked.

"Come on in," he said with the wave of his arm.

His wife was waiting a few feet behind him and looked very different than the last time I saw her. "Maeve, it's so good to see you," I said, stepping forward to hug her. "Hammer didn't mention you were pregnant. Congratulations! When is the baby due?"

She rubbed her belly. "Next month."

"We're having a girl." Hammer's smile stretched across his face.

"Yeah? I'm so happy for you both," I said, looking between the two.

"Please introduce us," Maeve said, taking another step forward.

"Maeve, Hammer, this is Pearl Fischer."

"It's nice to meet you," Maeve said, shaking Pearl's hand. "Fischer. Why does that name sound familiar?"

Pearl's face flushed, and Maeve looked at her husband.

"What?" she asked.

I turned to Hammer, who was staring at me.

Pearl straightened her shoulders. "It's okay. I'll tell her. My father, John Fischer, was one of your kidnappers."

Maeve raised a brow and glared at her husband. "I see."

"If you'd like me to leave—"

"Leave? You just got here. Drip, offer them something to eat." Maeve looked at us. "Are you hungry?"

She rubbed her belly a second time. "I am twenty-four hours a day, if you want to know the truth of it."

She put her arm through Pearl's, something that clearly shocked her. "Come with me; we'll have a chat."

"You, come with me," Hammer said, pointing at me as he headed off in the direction of the kitchen. "We'll give 'em some time for Maeve to convince Pearl she's welcome here."

"Mighty forgiving of your wife."

Hammer looked up from where he was pouring iced tea into glasses. "Nothing to forgive. Pearl had no part in Maeve's abduction."

"Still. Guilt by association."

"Nah. You don't see it that way, do you?"

"No, but—"

"Then, why the hell would Maeve?" He pulled a bottle of beer out of the fridge. "Want one?"

"I'm good. I'll have some tea, please."

"You got it. Now, let's see what I can make my two girls to eat."

It took me a minute to realize he was talking about his wife and baby. "A girl, huh?"

Hammer smiled the same way he had earlier. "Damn straight. Like her mama, our daughter will be named after all the Mary Maeves who came before her."

Mary Maeve Donoghue was renowned in Ireland, going as far back as the sixteen hundreds. Each eldest female descendant was named after her.

"It's nice to see you so happy."

"Nicer to feel it."

I envied him. Not only was he married, but Maeve and Hammer were meant to be together. I'd realized that the first time I saw her at his place. I gave him a lot of shit that day, but it was clear the two were soulmates. His wife's fire matched his own, and that was good for the attorney.

"Does she want to move back to Ireland?" I asked.

Hammer shook his head. "She wants Mary and however many more kids we have to spend time there, but she doesn't want to live there permanently. Uncle Money is here; don't forget that."

It was hard to remember, sometimes, that the man I answered to for my current mission was Maeve's brother. Up until I saw him interact with her, the guy seemed more robot than human. Harsh thinking, I knew, but it was true. No one I'd ever known was as matter-of-fact as Kellen "Money" McTiernan.

"How'd he get that code name?" I realized I'd never heard the story.

"He's some kind of mathematical genius. When he was up-and-coming, the NSA wanted him more than the CIA did, since he was also a forensic accounting specialist. Can't imagine him sitting in a back office somewhere, running numbers instead of what he's doing now."

Five years ago, I doubted anyone would've predicted Money's meteoric rise in the agency. On the other hand, the man had the backing of the Invincibles and another private intelligence firm, K19 Security Solutions. Both organizations counted several former CIA agents among their partners, myself included. Although I wasn't a partner. Wasn't even sure I wanted to be, not that anyone had asked.

I could afford the buy-in it would take. I certainly made more than enough money between my gig here at the ranch and as an Invincibles contractor, especially since I paid nothing for the house I lived in.

A couple of years ago, I invested in a piece of land with frontage on Lady Bird Lake, not too far from Austin. I wasn't sure I'd ever build on it since I never had time to even go there to fish.

"You just gonna stand there, or are you planning to help me?"

"Sorry, what?"

"Help. You know, cut up some vegetables, slice some cheese."

I looked down at the cutting board and knife he'd set in front of me. "Yeah, sorry. Got lost in thought for a minute."

"Pearl?"

"Nah. I'm thinking about selling my property on the lake."

"Never sell property if you don't have to. My grand-dad always said the more dirt you own, the wealthier you are. Even if you don't have a penny in your pocket."

"I'm not sure I'll ever do anything with it."

"My guess is it's already appreciated since you bought it. Hang on to it, and the value will keep goin' up. You don't need the money, Rip. Even I know that."

He was right. Maybe tomorrow, I'd take Pearl to see it. There weren't a lot of places I'd feel comfortable taking her off the ranch, but there, I would. First, it was a gated and exclusive community. Second, I hadn't bought just one lot; I'd bought three. That way, if I ever did build, I wouldn't have neighbors too close.

Hammer buying the three ranches he'd combined into one was what had given me the idea. However, he owned about ten times more acres of dirt than I did.

"Shall we go see how the ladies are faring?" he asked.

"Sure." While I tried to come off as nonchalant, the truth was I liked being around Pearl. She hadn't been staying with me much longer than a week, and I still knew I'd miss her when the time came for her to leave.

8

Pearl

"Your home is beautiful," I said when Maeve led me into a sitting room. Off to one side was a piano that I eyed longingly. There was one in the main hall on the compound, an upright, that I always wished I'd learned to play.

"Thank you, and come sit."

"Hammer said you're from Dublin." I took a seat across from her on one of the two small couches.

"Yes." She leaned back and rubbed her belly like I'd seen her do before.

"Do you miss it?"

She looked up at me almost as though she didn't understand the question. "I suppose if I do, I'll go and visit. Right now, I'm happy to be here in Texas. Hard to believe that a year ago I was so lost and now I have everything I never knew I wanted."

"You have a very grand home."

Maeve nodded. "That doesn't matter much to me. As they say, money doesn't buy love or happiness. Health, either."

"I wouldn't know. I've never had any. And by any, I mean none."

Maeve scrunched her eyes. "As I said, there are far more important things."

"I really didn't need it on the compound. It wasn't like there was anything I needed to buy. Now, though, Rip had Misty get me some new clothes, and I feel bad not contributing to that or to the food he provides. I've offered to earn my keep, but he hasn't come up with anything much yet, other than cooking and some cleaning."

"You said 'on the compound.' Tell me more."

I didn't want to be rude, but I also didn't want to talk about it. I doubted she really cared about the compound anyway. She probably wanted to know more about my father. "I lived there all my life."

"I know your father passed. I'm very sorry for your loss."

"Thank you, but you don't have to say that."

"Why ever not? It's how I feel. When my da passed, a few years ago, I missed him so much. Still do."

"My father kidnapped you."

"That doesn't change the fact that he raised you."

"I suppose."

"What about your mum? Is she still alive?"

I shook my head. "I never knew her."

"Aye. My own passed when I was just five. It's only recently I've begun having memories of her. I'm not certain if they're really memories or just things I've conjured in my brain. Pregnancy does funny things to you that way. And I can no longer see my feet."

Maeve laughed, and I did too.

"We've a lot in common, Pearl."

"We do?" The words came out sounding as shocked as I felt.

"Both lost our mums. Our dads too, but more recently. I want you to know I understand how disconcerting that feels. I've a half brother, but there were still times I felt a bit of an orphan. Now Hammer and this little one I can't wait to meet are my family. Someday, you'll know exactly how I feel."

I didn't say it out loud, but I doubted it. What man would ever want me? I wasn't pretty—I'd heard that often enough, whispered by the other women on the compound. I had no particular skills, and given I knew so little about the world outside the confines I'd grown up in, I wasn't very interesting either. Coupled with the fact that my father was a member of the Aryan Brotherhood of Texas and a criminal, I wasn't exactly a "catch."

"I know what you're thinking," Maeve said when I realized she was studying me. "And you're wrong."

Before I could ask what she meant, Rip and Hammer came in, carrying two large platters filled with food.

"I could've helped with that," I said, jumping up from the couch. It was really the only useful thing I knew how to do.

"Sit down and relax, Pearl," Rip said, winking at me. "It's okay to let others do things for you sometimes."

"He's right," said Maeve. "As my husband continues to remind me, once this bairn is born, I'll not have a minute to myself, nor one to relax. I've decided, after months of being stubborn, to listen to him."

I sat down and folded my hands in my lap. "If you need any help, I've taken care of lots and lots of babies on the compound." I bit my lip, realizing how uncomfortable I must be making the woman who had been so gracious to me. "I understand if you wouldn't want my help, though."

Maeve got up from the other couch, walked around the table, and sat beside me. "That is a wonderful idea, and I'd love to have your help. In fact, I could use help now if you have the time." She looked up at Rip and Hammer, who still stood, holding the platters of food.

"What are you waiting for, then? Set those down and go get the rest."

I laughed out loud when both men did as she said and hurried off in the direction they came from.

"They mind so well, don't they?" Maeve laughed too, then took my hand. "Tell me, what kinds of things do you like to do?"

I almost cried at her kindness. It felt so genuine. "I can cook and bake. I sew, but not as well as some of the other women on the compound."

"I can't sew at all, so you have me beat."

"I can clean, too, or help in the barns and fields."

"Let's focus on what's to be done here at the house first. We have someone who takes care of the cleaning, but I'm sure she'd welcome the extra hands. I am so hopeless in the kitchen my husband handles most of the cooking. We can start there if you'd like."

"I'll have to see what Rip needs me for first, if that's okay. I made him the same offer."

"We'll ask him together."

The men returned with plates, napkins, and drinks, which they set on the table in front of us, where they'd already left the food.

"Anything else missing?" Hammer asked his wife.

"I could go for a sweet, but I'm afraid I polished all of those off last night."

"I can make some cookies later if you'd like. Or now, if you have the ingredients."

"I'll be thrilled if you would, but later. Now, I want to continue our chat."

Maeve told Rip and Hammer about the offer she'd made me and that she hoped to be able to work out a schedule that wouldn't interfere with my other responsibilities. She stood and returned to the couch across from me, and Hammer sat beside her. Rip took her place next to me.

"You don't need to worry about stuff at my house. I did most of it before, and I can do it again. I wouldn't mind more blueberry pancakes for breakfast every once in a while, though." He turned to me, winked, and smiled.

"*Blueberry pancakes*? Do you really know how to make them?" Maeve gasped.

"The best I've ever had," said Rip.

I was close to crying again. While Mr. Robinson and Ms. Shay had been kind to me, it was a rarity in my life, especially since my father died. These people hardly knew me, yet they treated me better than others who'd known me since I was a child.

"I won't let any of you down," I said, blinking away my tears.

"What's this now?" said Maeve. "No tears! I've the market on those. Pregnancy does that. The other thing is, I have to use the loo a hundred times a day."

When she stood, Hammer did too. "I'll get more tea."

After they'd both left, Rip stretched his arm behind me and rested it on the back of the couch. "Feeling any better?"

"She's so nice."

"I agree."

I turned to face him. "You are too. Thank you for all you're doing for me. Know that I will repay you, and even though you said I don't have responsibilities,

I intend to cook and bake and clean, just like I said I would."

"That isn't why I'm helping you, Pearl."

"I know. Mr. Robinson asked you to, and I appreciate it so much."

"That isn't why, either."

"Why, then?"

Before he could respond, Maeve and Hammer were back.

9

Rip

After we'd finished "snacking" so much I considered it a meal, Hammer suggested Maeve and Pearl sit out on the patio and enjoy the sun while he and I cleaned up.

"I like her. She's not at all what I expected."

I agreed, but I was curious. "What did you expect?"

"That she'd be more timid. There are signs of it, but not as much as I'd anticipated. I can't imagine the life she must've led."

"She was whipped at a hitching post," I blurted.

Hammer studied me.

"I don't know that for certain, but the way she reacted…"

"We need to shut those fuckers down permanently," he said under his breath as he handed me a dish towel. "How's that going, by the way?"

I looked out the window to make sure Pearl and Maeve were still out on the patio.

"Vex didn't have any luck in Idaho. He didn't want to push too hard and draw suspicion, but no one knew a thing about John Fischer or his daughter."

"He briefed me that first night about what Scottie overheard. There's gotta be a reason the assholes think she's of value. Or of interest, anyway."

"She has no idea Fischer wasn't her dad."

"That much was obvious." Hammer dried his hands after he'd finished with the dishes and leaned up against the counter. "You know, there might be a way to figure out who is."

"DNA?"

"Bingo. Most of these scumbags are probably in the system by now. If not them, someone who's a close enough relative."

Law enforcement had made significant progress with cold case files in the last ten years since DNA testing became something anyone with twenty-five bucks could do. The main inroads had been made in rape and murder investigations.

"Before you go down that road, my opinion is you should be honest with her about Fischer."

I agreed, and I intended to. I almost had earlier today when we rode out. Something told me it was too soon, though.

"As far as her working for Maeve and me, we'll pay her a fair wage. For now, of course, it will need to be in cash."

Finding out who she really was would become more important the more assimilated she became to life outside the compound. For now, things like getting identification and having a bank account would be impossible. Hell, I bet she didn't even know how to drive.

I didn't understand women who chose to join cults, or even stay there, but everything I'd read said, like with women in abusive relationships, nothing was as simple as leaving. Someone like Pearl had never known anything else.

"You good with this, Rip?"

I'd been watching the animated way she and Maeve were talking, but turned to look at him. "What do you mean?"

"Havin' somebody livin' in your house?"

Better than I'd admit. If I told Hammer how much I liked having her there, he'd think I was nuts. I hardly knew her. "If I wasn't okay, I wouldn't have done it."

He nodded.

"Vex *suggested* I take her to the safe house, but that didn't feel right to me."

"Gotta go with your gut."

The expression was one I heard a lot and said even more.

"They're on the way in," I told him when I looked out and saw them walking toward the door.

"My guess is my wife has already covered hours and pay." Hammer laughed. "She has a helluva lot more experience with that kind of thing than I do. Outside of the ranch, where you're my main employee, Fury is the first person I've brought on at the firm."

"Really? Not even an assistant?"

"I have one client. What the hell do I need an assistant for?"

I laughed. "Good point."

Hammer looked at his watch. "Maeve will be getting tired."

"Roger that. We'll be on our way."

"You said you're square with Fury, right?"

"I think she was long since done with me."

He patted my back. "Good. I don't like havin' to get in the middle of shit like that."

It looked like he had something else to say, so I waited.

"If it gets to be too much, having Pearl at your place, she can stay here."

"I appreciate the offer." I doubted there were too many things I'd meant less, and I sure as hell couldn't explain why I felt that way.

"Wanna go for a ride?" I asked Pearl once she and I had said our goodbyes to Hammer and Maeve.

"Are you sure you don't want me to get started on dinner?"

I patted my belly. "I don't think I could eat it if you did. I'm pretty full from what Hammer referred to as a snack."

She laughed. "Me too."

"You're nice to be around, Pearl."

"So are you, Rip."

We were almost to the ranch gate when I saw a familiar car heading in our direction. When it got close,

I slowed to a stop and rolled my window down. "Hey, Fury," I said when she did the same.

"Hey, Rip." She looked beyond me. "Hey, Rip's friend."

"This is Pearl."

She waved. "Hi, Pearl."

"Hello, ma'am."

"Ma'am?" Fury laughed. "I'm still not used to being back in Texas. Everybody calling me ma'am makes me feel like an old lady."

"We were headed out on a drive. You meeting with Hammer?"

"Yes. Invincibles—err—you know…business."

"Yep." I tipped my hat. "You take care, Fury."

"You too, Rip."

I rolled up the window and pulled away.

"That's your woman? She's beautiful."

"First of all, she's not my woman. Second, she isn't half as pretty as you are, Pearl." When I saw how pale her face went and that she turned her head away, I regretted my words. "I'm sorry if I made you feel uncomfortable."

She continued staring out the window.

"Pearl?"

"I'm sorry. I heard you, and it's okay." While trying to keep one eye on the road, I kept the other on her. Finally, she looked at me. "I liked it."

When I pulled through the gate of the development after punching my code into the keypad, I realized I didn't remember the last time I'd driven out this way.

"It's pretty here," Pearl, who had been quiet the rest of the drive, said.

"I thought so."

"Who lives here?"

"Lots of people I don't know," I told her as we drove by more houses than had been here before.

"Do you live here?"

"Not yet."

I went around two bends in the road, and the view of the lake stretched out in front of us. I pulled onto the grass and as far forward as I could. "Do you like to fish?"

"Fish?"

I chuckled. "You know, throw a line into the water and see what you catch?"

"I've never done it."

"I'll show you." Even though I hadn't done it recently, I still kept a tackle box and a couple of poles in the back of the SUV, just in case. I grabbed the blanket I also kept there and led Pearl to the water's edge.

"Are you squeamish?" I asked.

She cocked her head.

"Will you get sick to your stomach if I catch one? Sometimes, it gets a little bit bloody. Not too much, though."

She shrugged. "Probably no worse than killing a chicken, right?"

"Have you had to do a lot of that?"

"Some."

"This will be a lot less gruesome than that." I got the two poles set up with lures and handed one to her. I showed her how to cast the line, and after two or three tries, she had it down.

"You're one of those people, aren't you?" I said, knowing as soon as I did that it was the wrong thing—again. "What I meant by that is you're one of those people who are really good at everything they try."

Pearl made a face at me. "Very funny."

I held up my hands. "I meant it. Look," I pointed at her line. "Reel it in."

"Do what?"

I stood behind her and wrapped my arms around her so I could show her. "See? Just turn this handle and bring it in."

I couldn't help but breathe in the scent of her. It was fresh and pure, like a meadow in springtime, when the sun had been shining down on it. I stepped around her and held the fish up once she'd reeled it in far enough. "You got a big one too! Look at that."

"What do we do with it now?"

"This here is catch-and-release fishing," I said as I removed the lure and tossed the largemouth bass back in the water.

"What's the point if you just let them go?"

"It's relaxing."

She raised both eyebrows and cast her line again. After an hour, Pearl had caught and released six to my zero.

"Are you sure we can't keep any?" she asked when she caught number seven, which looked bigger than the others.

I shook my head. "Why do you want to?"

"Fishing made me hungry."

I chuckled. "Me too."

"I don't think I like fish, though."

"No? I love a good fried catfish."

"I've never had it."

"Catfish or any fish?" I asked.

"Any fish."

"Then, I know just the place for us to get some." It would take some finagling on my part, but I thought I could make it work.

We were about fifteen minutes from the ranch when I pulled over and placed a call.

"Hey, Rebel," I said when the woman who helped out behind the bar and in the kitchen at the Long Branch when needed answered. With both Maeve and Hammer taking some time off before the baby was born, my guess was Rebel and her husband, Edge, who was one of the Invincibles partners, were there pretty much every day.

"Hey, Rip. What can I do for you, sugar?"

"You don't happen to have two orders of catfish you could package up for me as takeout, do you?"

"Sure do. You want coleslaw and potato salad with those?"

I looked at Pearl, who could easily hear everything Rebel had said. She nodded her head enthusiastically.

"That'll be perfect."

"Give me about fifteen minutes, and I'll have 'em ready."

"I'll swing by the family entrance and grab them."

I ended the call and was about to put the SUV in gear when I noticed a group of motorcycles headed our way. Rather than pull out, I waited a couple of minutes to give them time to pass. I wasn't worried about any of them seeing into my vehicle since the windows were tinted pretty dark, but I wanted to get a good look at them, as much as I could see by the light of the moon anyway.

"Let me know if you recognize any of these bikes," I said when they were almost to us. "Or anyone riding them."

"All of them," she said as they drove by in groups.

"ABT?"

"Yes."

Rather than follow, I spun the SUV around and went in the opposite direction. Once I turned off the main road, I called Rebel back. "ABT headed your way," I said when she answered. "You want me to call the sheriff?"

"A couple of them passed Tres on his way in, so he's way ahead of you, Rip, but thanks for the heads-up."

"I'm gonna have to take a pass on the catfish, darlin'. I'm really sorry about that."

"Hammer is headed out with a couple of T-bones. You want me to have him bring your dinners to the ranch with him?"

"If he wouldn't mind."

Rebel laughed and ended the call.

I looked over at Pearl, who was wide-eyed and white as a sheet.

"It's okay. You're safe with me. You know that, right?"

"They're out looking for me. I can feel it."

"Well, they aren't going to find you." Seconds later, we pulled through the gates of the Hammered Dubliner—a place we wouldn't be leaving again anytime soon.

Rather than going to my house, I pulled up in front of Hammer's and called to say I was here, waiting.

"You heard we had company at the Branch," he said.

"Saw them myself."

"We'll talk more when I get there. Go on inside. I'll let Maeve know you and Pearl will be having dinner with us. We might need to rethink the plan."

"This is all my fault," said Pearl. "He doesn't want me here anymore."

"I don't know what you think is your fault, and unless you're some kind of mind reader, you don't know what Hammer is thinking, either. We need to head inside in just a minute, but first, there's something I want to talk to you about."

I knew she didn't want to go in. I also knew she would anyway. Either way, I was about to reveal to her exactly who I was. I had to, because even though I couldn't read minds, either, I still knew Hammer was going to suggest we relocate.

She turned her body so she was facing me. "Go ahead."

"Before this goes any further, I need you to know I'm not *exactly* who you think I am."

She folded her arms. "Who are you?"

"My name is Rip, or Zane, like I told you. I just never was a part of the Nazi Freedom Riders."

Pearl smiled.

"What?"

"I knew that inside of five minutes of meeting you."

I smiled too. "Yeah? How? Do I look too soft to have been one of them?"

"You're too nice." I could see the wheels turning in her head. "Mr. Robinson and Ms. Shay aren't who they said they were, either."

"That's right."

"I think deep down I knew that too. Why are you telling me now?"

"So it's easier for Hammer and me to talk freely about our next course of action."

"What about Maeve?"

"You might not believe this, but…Maeve's brother is actually the head of the CIA."

Again, her eyes opened wide. "She's Irish."

"He isn't. He's actually her half brother."

"Is that who you work for?"

"Indirectly. I work for a company called the Invincibles."

"Your woman said that name."

I raised a brow. "She's *not* my woman."

"She wants to be."

"You saw her for thirty seconds. What makes you say something like that?"

She turned her head away so I couldn't see her face. "Any woman would want to be."

"Pearl—" Before I could say another word, she got out of the SUV. I did too and headed her off before she got up the steps to the front door. "Don't run away from me," I said when she tried to skirt past me.

I put my hands on her arms. "Pearl?"

"What?"

"Look at me."

She sure as hell didn't want to, but eventually, she did anyway.

"Any man would want you to be his too."

"You're just saying that because I said it first."

"Am I? Are you reading my mind now too?"

"You don't mean it."

"You're wrong." Before I could do something stupid, like show her exactly how wrong she was, Hammer's vehicle pulled up next to mine. "You head on inside, and I'll help him bring the food in."

She took off as soon as I released her.

"Hey, Pearl?"

She looked over her shoulder at me.

"We're going to finish this conversation later."

"What conversation?" Hammer asked when I walked over to grab some of the take-out boxes from his hands.

"She knows I'm not a former Nazi Freedom Rider."

"I see. What else?"

"That Vex and Scottie aren't who they say they are, either."

"You must trust her."

"I do and—"

Hammer held up his hand. "You don't have to say another word. If you do, that's good enough for me. It makes the conversation I want to have a helluva lot easier."

"Which is exactly why I told her."

10

Pearl

Maeve hollered for me to come in when I knocked.

"How are you doing?" she asked, coming out of the dining room.

My head was spinning, but not just because I'd seen some of the ABT guys.

"Come and sit."

I nodded, and she led me into the side room where the piano was and motioned for me to be seated. She did the same.

"You're safe here. You know that, right?"

"I do. Rip told me he isn't who I thought he was."

"I'm glad. I had a feeling he would. How are you feeling about it?"

Before I could answer, Rip and Hammer came in the front door. "You want to eat in there or in the dining room?" her husband asked.

"In the breakfast nook. We'll join you in a minute." When they left, her gaze met mine. "Go ahead."

"I told him I already knew."

"I figured as much. You're smart, Pearl."

"I don't know about that. I mean, it was kind of obvious." I chuckled and Maeve laughed. "He asked if it was because he was too 'soft.'"

"What did you say?"

"I told him it was because he's too nice."

Maeve's expression turned more serious. "He's a good man, and he *will* keep you safe."

"I believe that."

"Good. Now, let's eat and see what he and my husband have drummed up."

I followed Maeve into the kitchen, where Rip and Hammer had napkins and silverware on the table and the food on the counter for us to dish onto plates.

"Oh, I *love* catfish," Maeve exclaimed.

"You're welcome to have some of mine."

"You wouldn't mind? I'm happy to share my steak with you too."

While I wasn't sure what to expect from the fish, I had to admit it was very good. The steak, though, was the best I'd ever had. Not that I'd had much. The men at the compound had steak a lot more than the women did, and what we had didn't even look like what we were eating. For one, it was always cooked to the point where it was gray and dry rather than juicy and pink.

Every so often, I'd look up at Rip. Each time I did, his eyes met mine. I wished I knew what he was thinking. I didn't regret what I'd said to him earlier. I meant it. Any woman would want him to be hers. He wasn't just handsome; he was patient, kind, and thoughtful too. Even my father hadn't paid as much attention to me as Rip did. If I was pensive, he'd ask what I was thinking about, and so often, I'd find him studying me. Kind of like a puzzle he was trying to solve.

Each day we were together at his house was easier than the day before. I couldn't imagine life being any better, and whenever I thought about having to leave someday, my eyes filled with tears and I forced myself to think about something else.

"Did you see what Rebel sent along with dinner?" Hammer asked Maeve.

She looked over at the counter. "I didn't. What?"

"A whole pecan pie along with some brownies."

Maeve clapped her hands. "A woman after my heart."

"Maybe it's your husband after your heart since I ordered both." Hammer winked at her.

My cheeks flushed at their flirting. More when I looked up at Rip, who smiled and winked at me like Hammer had to Maeve.

"You two go relax in the living room, and we'll be in shortly," Hammer said after we'd finished dessert.

"Please let me help tonight. I didn't lift a finger when I was here earlier," I said, standing and taking my plate and Maeve's over to the sink.

"I'll help too," Rip offered.

"Hammer, let's go out to the patio, and you can light the fire pit," Maeve suggested.

"We'll be out soon," Rip said, grabbing more of the dishes. When he brought them over to the sink where I was washing them, his arm brushed against mine. Rather than apologize or move away, he stayed where he was. I didn't move my arm either.

When we finished cleaning up, we joined Maeve and Hammer out by the fire. Rip motioned for me to sit in one of the two-seaters, like our hosts were. Again, our arms brushed, and neither of us moved away.

I wished he'd put his arm around me so I could rest my head on his shoulder like Maeve was with her husband. Or that he'd stroke my hair and lean over every so often to kiss my forehead, like Hammer was. Just our arms touching, though, made me want to hold my breath and wish this moment would never end.

"Rip, I think we should discuss your next course of action. You and Pearl are more than welcome to stay here at the ranch, but I'm wondering if it might be a good idea for you to get out of Texas for the time being," said Hammer.

"I was thinking the same thing."

"Got anywhere in mind?"

Rip nodded. "Roaring Fork Ranch has several guest cabins on the property. I know since I helped build them."

"That's an excellent idea. I hadn't thought of it."

"Did you have somewhere else in mind?" Rip asked.

Hammer nodded. "Smoke's place in Tennessee, but I think Roaring Fork would be better."

"I'll reach out to Buck Wheaton in the morning."

"Pearl?" said Maeve. "How would you feel about leaving for a bit?"

I took a deep breath and let it out slowly. "I don't know what y'all are talking about, but I don't want you to be in danger because of me, so I'll do whatever you think is best." I hoped and prayed that didn't mean going back to the compound, but so far, it didn't sound that way.

"You'll need to take the Invincibles' jet," said Hammer. "Let me know when you think you want to head out, and I'll make the arrangements."

"Thank you," said Rip. "I hadn't considered the logistics, but you're right. We'll need to fly private rather than commercial."

"Fly?" I gasped, wishing I hadn't blurted it out that way.

"The Roaring Fork Ranch I mentioned is in Colorado. It'll take under three hours if we fly. If we drive, it'll be more like fifteen."

"I wouldn't recommend it anyway," Hammer said, looking directly at Rip.

"I agree."

Maeve cleared her throat. "While I have an abundantly clear idea of what you and Rip think, Drip, I asked Pearl what she thinks of all this."

Hammer smiled. "Yes, Dublin."

"He calls her Dublin because she's from Ireland. She calls him Drip because the ranch is in Dripping Springs," Rip leaned over and whispered.

I'd wondered when I heard her call him that earlier.

"Pearl?" Maeve repeated.

"As I said, I'll do whatever Rip thinks is best."

"Do you have any questions?" she asked.

I smiled. "About a hundred."

"While these two have your best interest at heart, I want to be sure you're okay with leaving the state."

"I'm fine. Really," I assured her. As I'd said, I didn't understand much of what Rip and Hammer were talking about, but in *my* heart, I knew their only goal was to keep me safe.

Maeve continued to study me, but I didn't know what else I could say.

"Have you been on a plane before?" she asked.

"No, ma'am."

As soon as I'd said the words, Rip reached his arm around behind me and rubbed my shoulder. "Your first experience will definitely be luxury all the way since we'll be traveling via my employer's private plane."

"It is quite lovely," said Maeve. "You'll be spoiled."

I nodded but felt like I was listening to a conversation in another language.

"I don't know about the rest of you, but I'm having trouble keeping my eyes open. Take me to bed, husband," said Maeve, nudging Hammer.

"We'll be on our way." Rip stood and held his hand out to help me up.

Maeve walked over to us and took my hands in hers. "Stop by in the morning, before you leave."

"We will," Rip told her.

"Good night, then." Before I could walk away, she pulled me into a hug like Ms. Shay had the last time I saw her. If she hadn't told us to stop by before we left, I would've worried I'd never see her again. I wondered now if I would see Mr. Robinson or Ms. Shay again.

"That was a lot to take in," Rip said once we were back in the SUV. "Once we're at the house, you can ask me any questions you want to."

"Thank you…" I'd almost said sir, but stopped myself. "I wouldn't know where to begin."

"I have one idea. I can show you photos of where we're going."

"I'd like that."

By the time we got to the house, I was having a hard time keeping my eyes open as well. "Would it be possible for you to show me in the morning, instead?"

"Feeling tired?" he asked.

"Very."

"Come here," he said as I was about to walk into the bedroom.

"What?"

Like I wished he would when we were sitting by the fire, Rip pulled me into his arms so my head rested on his chest. "I promise this is going to be okay," he said before leaning down and kissing my temple. "Get some sleep, and we'll take this one step at a time tomorrow."

I nodded when he backed up. "Thank you."

"Sweet dreams, Pearl," he said as he walked away.

Did he know they'd be of him, just like they had been over the last couple of nights?

When I climbed into bed a few minutes later, I hugged Mojo close to me. Riding on a plane for the first time wasn't what kept me tossing and turning. Instead, it was the conversation Rip said he and I would continue later, the one after he'd told me any man would want me to be his.

11

Rip

Before going to my side of the house, I stopped in the kitchen to get two of the oatmeal chocolate-chip cookies Pearl had made yesterday. She was absolutely right when she said they needed more butter. I wouldn't have been able to pinpoint the difference if she hadn't; all I knew was they reminded me more of the ones my nana used to make.

I looked out the window after pouring myself a glass of milk. Here I was, thinking about cookies when there was a helluva lot more I should be thinking about. For starters, the conversation Pearl and I began when we arrived at Hammer's place. The one during which she'd said any woman would want me to be her man and continued with my saying any man would want her to be his too. The same conversation I'd told her we'd continue later.

The truth of it was I'd felt an underlying attraction to Pearl from the moment I shook her hand in that parking garage. The more I got to know her, the more it grew. Was it just responsibility I felt? I didn't think so. Responsibility and attraction were very different emotions, something I believed I could decipher between. Particularly when I considered some of the other instances over the course of my career when I'd been responsible for protecting someone.

I'd given a lot of thought to my growing attraction to the woman in my care. Not just today, but every night before I fell asleep. I could say with certainty that I'd never felt the way I did when I looked at her. Or when we were together, just doing something as mundane as the dishes. Or sitting beside each other over a meal. Especially today, when I'd wrapped my arms around her to show her how to reel her fishing line in.

However, it wasn't all about me and how I was feeling. I knew Pearl was attracted to me, maybe better than she knew herself. I'd see her breath hitch, her cheeks flush, or her pupils dilate. She was just as affected while we were fishing as I'd been.

There was still the chance or the possibility that it was the first time she'd actually allowed herself to *feel* attraction. Did she see me only as the man who'd saved her? Was it more than just the freedom to feel she was experiencing? Or was it the totality of the world that had been opened up to her—the one so unlike anything she'd ever known?

Tomorrow, that world would open up even more, and it would be like a fairy tale. Most people lived their whole lives without ever traveling on a private plane, to another state, or visiting a place like the Roaring Fork Ranch, truly one of the most beautiful places on earth as far as I was concerned.

While it was becoming increasingly difficult for me to stop myself from touching her, I had to rein myself in, at least until she and I could have a frank conversation about the things we were both experiencing. I owed her that much honesty.

"Rip?"

I was still looking out the window when I heard her say my name from behind me. I could see her reflection, though. Without turning to look, I knew the light from the hallway would pass through the sheerness of her nightgown and I'd be able to see the outline of her body. Maybe more than just the outline.

"Go back to bed, Pearl. We have a long day ahead of us tomorrow."

She took a step closer to me. "I can't sleep."

I raised my head to the ceiling and closed my eyes. "You need to try."

She took another step. "Are you angry with me about something?"

I opened my eyes, and our gazes met in the window's reflection.

"I'm not."

"Then, why won't you look at me?"

"Because if I turn around, I'm going to be able to see right through your nightgown, darlin'. I don't think you'd like that, now, would you?"

Her breath hitched. "I would."

"Pearl." I sighed her name more than spoke it when she took the final step that brought her close enough to touch if I simply turned around.

"You said any man would want me to be his. Did you mean any man but you?"

"No. That isn't what I meant."

"Then, why—"

"Go to bed, Pearl. This is the last time I'm going to say it."

"What will happen if I don't?"

"Something neither of us is ready for." I could see her tears in the window as if I were looking at her.

I breathed a sigh of relief when she turned around and left. I hated that I'd made her cry, but it was the lesser evil. The alternative would be so much worse.

When I heard the bedroom door close, I pulled out my phone, turned the lights off throughout the house, and made my way to my own room in the dark.

Pearl wasn't in the kitchen when I got up the next morning, so I made enough breakfast for both of us. When a half hour passed without her joining me, I walked down the hallway and knocked on her door.

"Breakfast is ready," I said, growing increasingly uncomfortable with every second that passed without her responding. "Pearl?"

I was about to open the door to check on her when my phone vibrated in my back pocket.

If you're looking for Pearl, she just showed up here at the house, read the text message Hammer sent.

On my way, I responded.

Give it some more time. I'll message again when you should head over.

Is she okay?

She and Maeve went to have girl talk.

Roger that. Thanks, Hammer.

Knowing she wasn't in the room, I opened the door. I'd respected her privacy since she arrived, and hadn't entered her room after the first night when I followed her in.

As I probably should've expected, her bed was perfectly made, almost as though it had never been slept in, and not a thing was out of place. I opened the second drawer of the dresser and ran my hand over her clothes, folded as neatly as they would be on the shelves of a store.

Part of me wished I had found it in complete disarray. That after escaping the confines of the compound, she felt free enough to leave the bed unmade, to scatter her clothes around the room. I wondered if she'd ever feel that free.

I thought about our first ride out, the morning after I'd brought her to the ranch, and how I'd motioned to the expanse of the horizon and told her what I saw was freedom. That was what she needed more than anything.

Not to go from one "man's care" to another—meaning from the men on the compound to me.

The articles I'd read about cult survivors and the processes they went through after leaving them played over in my head.

Healing. Recovery. Empowerment. None of those things could come *from* me. Pearl needed to work through each step on her own. I could be there to give the little pushes she might need, but I couldn't take her hand and lead her.

While I waited to hear back from Hammer, I sent Buck a text, asking him to get in touch when he got my message. Like with most messages sent via HALE, he responded almost immediately.

"Hey, Rip. How the hell are you? My brothers and I were just talking about you yesterday."

"You were? All bad things, I imagine."

Buck laughed. "What can I do for you this morning?"

"I have a favor to ask."

"Whatever it is, you got it."

"You might want to hear me out first."

"If it would make you feel better, but I can tell you, my answer will still be yes."

I told Buck about the ABT and Vex being under-cover with them, then about Maeve McTiernan's kidnapping and the aftermath, with a sidebar about her being Money's half sister.

"You are welcome here anytime, man. You're family. As far as the asset protection goes, I haven't been read in on this mission yet. Would Money approve you doing that now?"

"My mission, and you're on the team, so absolutely."

"I heard Hammer got married, that ol' rascal," he said after I finished briefing him on Pearl Fischer.

"Maeve is pregnant too."

"Damn, that makes me happy. Our little one is just about a month old."

"Well, hell, Buck, congratulations. How does time fly that fast? How is Stella doin'?"

"Best mother I've ever seen, if you wanna know the truth."

"I am not," I heard her say in the background.

"Rip is coming to stay on the ranch in one of the guest cabins," Buck told her. I couldn't hear her response, but Stella and I had always gotten along well.

"Hey, Buck, boy or girl?" Since when did I give a shit?

"Little boy. For now, we call him Buckaroo."

Whereas hearing something like that might've made me throw up in my mouth a little over a month ago, for some reason, hearing about Buck's baby made me wish I had a little Ripper. "Happy for you, my friend."

"Thanks. I got a diaper to change, so I need to run. Send me your itinerary when you know it."

"Will do, and thanks again."

"I'll have my siblings plan a welcome-home dinner too."

Home. It was interesting that Buck used that word. For a long time, I thought the ranch that had been in his family—the Roaring Fork—might become my semi-permanent home. Either that or some other piece of property near it in Crested Butte, Colorado.

Instead, I ended up in Dripping Springs, Texas, with Hammer. If I hadn't, it's doubtful I would've been assigned to this mission or that I would've met Pearl.

Pearl. She was upset with me enough that she'd left my place and walked to Hammer and Maeve's this morning. However, I stood by everything I said and did last night.

I was about to send Hammer another message when I heard from him. *You're invited up for breakfast,* his text read.

On my way, I responded for the second time this morning.

12

Pearl

Walking from Rip's house to Maeve and Hammer's probably wasn't the smartest thing I'd ever done. First, it was a lot farther than I thought. Second, they might not even be home. Worse, they might still be asleep.

When I got close enough to see Maeve outside on the patio, I breathed a sigh of relief. More so when she waved.

"I'm glad you're here," she said when I joined her.

"You are?"

"Of course I am. I told you to stop by this morning before you left."

"I thought maybe it was too early."

"Not at all. Unless I've worked the night before, I'm always up with the sunrise. Come inside. Have you had breakfast?"

"Not yet."

"Perfect. You can teach me how to make your blueberry pancakes."

Maeve asked me what ingredients we'd need and took me into a pantry that was half the size of the storeroom at the compound that held food for everyone who lived there.

"Is this just for you and Hammer?" I asked, realizing it might've sounded rude as soon as I said it.

Maeve smiled. "It is. Isn't that terrible?"

I looked down at the floor. "No. I'm so sorry—"

"Stop."

I raised my head.

"You can say whatever is on your mind to me, and I will do the same. Understood?"

"Yes, ma'am."

"Maeve."

"Yes, Maeve."

"Good. Now, show me what we need. I'll bring it to the kitchen, and you can tell me what happened between you and Rip that made you walk two miles to see me first thing in the morning."

When I said I'd make the pancakes, she ordered me to sit instead. "I want to be able to make them myself while you're away," she explained. "Write out the recipe, then start talking."

Write out the recipe? It seemed simple enough to me, but then I'd been making them since I first learned to cook. Ms. Opal was who'd taught me to make them, along with many other things, including oatmeal chocolate-chip cookies. Since my memories of her were good ones—something rare for me—that's the name I put at the top of the piece of paper Maeve handed me—*Ms. Opal's Blueberry Pancakes.*

While she added the ingredients to the bowl and stirred the batter, I began by telling her about Rip stopping to talk to the woman when we were leaving the ranch to go fishing.

"Ah, Fury, right?"

"Yes."

"I'll admit the first time she and I met, I was sure she and Hammer had had sex. I let my temper get the best of me and left. Rather than storming off on foot, though, I got in my truck and drove all the way to Austin. But that's another story. Go on."

"I can't drive."

Maeve laughed. "Or you would have done."

"Probably. Anyway, I told him I thought she wanted to be his woman."

"Hmm. I don't know her well, but I can't quite imagine Fury wanting to be with Rip that way."

"When he asked me if I could read her mind…or something like that…I told him I thought any woman would want to be his."

"I see." Maeve stopped stirring the batter. "Well done, Pearl. What did he say?"

"That any man would want me to be his."

Maeve clapped her hands. "Oh, I love this story. What happened next?"

"Hammer drove up, and Rip said we'd continue the conversation later." Maeve put the griddle on the stove and turned on the heat. "You want it nice and hot," I added.

"Got it. Okay, so my husband arrived at the worst possible moment. With you so far. What happened after you got home?"

"I told him I was really tired and was going to bed. You want to keep the batter pour to a quarter of a cup or less," I said when she got out a ladle.

Maeve nodded and got out a measuring cup instead. "Okay, so you told him you were going to bed, but it didn't end there, did it?"

I shook my head. "I got ready for bed, then went looking for him."

"Bloody hell! This is getting good. Hang on. Let me get the rest of these on the griddle, then you can go on."

I watched as she measured out four perfect pancakes. "Once they bubble on top and get dry around the edges, it's time to flip them."

"All right, then. What happened next?"

"I found him in the kitchen, staring out the window."

"And?"

"He told me to go back to bed."

Maeve bit her bottom lip. "I see."

"He wouldn't even turn around and look at me."

"Well, he wouldn't do, now, would he?"

"What do you mean?"

"What were you wearing? Anything?"

I gasped and almost choked on my saliva. "Of course I was wearing something. I had on a nightgown."

"What was under it?"

"My panties."

"Got the picture. He wouldn't turn around, because he didn't want you to see his body's reaction. You know what I'm talking about, yeah?"

I knew my cheeks were beet red. "Yes."

"Next?"

"He told me again to go to bed, and I did."

"Then you woke up this morning, couldn't face him, and walked here."

"Yes, and you need to flip those."

"Right. Sorry. My mind is on you and Rip now."

I stood and walked around the island. "Here, I'll finish. You sit." I made eight more pancakes and put two on a plate for each of us. "Should we let Hammer know breakfast is ready?"

Maeve already had a forkful in her mouth and shook her head. "I may eat all of them, so we best not until we're sure we have enough."

I laughed. "I can make more."

"Good, but first, sit down with me and eat."

Maeve ate six more pancakes, but I stopped at two. I was about to get up to make more when she put her hand on my arm.

"Now that I'm full to the brim of the best pancakes I've ever had—I agree with Rip on that one—I'll tell you what I think about the two of you. Leave the dishes. We'll come back and do them."

"I hate to interrupt you two, but the plane is at Austin-Bergstrom. Rip and Pearl are going to have to leave soon," said Hammer, coming in from outside.

"We're almost finished, yes?" Maeve asked me.

"Yes."

"Invite him up for breakfast," she said before leading me out to the patio. It was warm enough that I could probably fall asleep in the sun, especially since I hadn't slept that well last night.

"Pearl, how old are you?"

As bizarre as it sounded, I wasn't quite sure. "Twenty-eight," I said, instead of trying to explain something I couldn't.

"While I'm a couple of years younger than you are, my life experience is vastly different. The things you need to ask yourself about your feelings for Rip would be the same regardless of your age."

"What things?"

"For starters, Rip rescued you."

"Actually, Mr. Robinson and Ms. Shay did that."

Maeve tilted her head. "Those are semantics, and you know it. Rip is the person keeping you safe, yes?"

I had to concede that much. "You're right."

"That's your first question. Is the attraction you're feeling for him because he makes you feel safe?"

In part, yes, but I didn't believe that was all it was. The first morning when Rip came into the kitchen, I felt things I never had before. I wasn't sure I'd ever experienced the kind of attraction for a man I did with him. "I don't think it's only for that reason."

Maeve smiled. "Good. Next question. Are you certain you're ready for what happens between a man and a woman, even before you toss sex into the mix?"

"I don't know what that means."

"Which part?" Maeve asked.

"The part before we toss sex in."

"Flirting, letting him know you're interested. I suppose you did do that last night." Her gaze on me felt as though it became more intent. "Pay close attention to your feelings, Pearl. If the answers to these questions—and the others I know you ask yourself—are that you understand the natural things you're feeling are genuine, then don't hold back."

"Show him how I feel?"

"Talk to him about it, at the very least." Maeve and I both looked in the direction of the sound when we heard a vehicle headed in our direction. "Here he is now," she announced unnecessarily.

13

Rip

While I was still too far away to be able to see Pearl's eyes clearly, I felt their intensity from inside my truck and sensed whatever "girl talk" she and Maeve had had, did not result in Pearl backing away from what she'd started last night.

My natural reaction to such knowledge should be to retreat instead. Yet, seeing her, made me want to do the opposite. I wanted to bound up the steps that led from the driveway, pull her into my arms, and tell her never to leave the way she had this morning. The other thing I felt compelled to do was kiss her like I'd dreamed about last night.

I got out of my truck and watched as Maeve went into the house. Pearl stayed where she was.

"Good morning," I said once I reached the stairs. "I missed having coffee and breakfast with you."

"I felt like taking a walk," she responded when I was close enough to her that I could reach out and touch her face with my fingertip. Not that I did.

"Was that the only reason? Just that you felt like taking a walk?"

"No."

"I'm sorry if I embarrassed you last night."

Pearl's cheeks pinkened, but otherwise, her shoulders remained square, and she didn't avert her gaze. "I'm sorry too, and before you start, you don't need to explain."

"I wasn't going to. Hammer said I was invited for breakfast."

"Yeah?"

"Yeah." I slowly nodded.

"I can make more pancakes." When she turned, presumably to go inside, I reached out and took her hand.

"Not yet."

"I don't want to talk about it."

Without letting go, I snaked my opposite arm around her waist, loving how she felt truly in my arms for the first time. "Am I making you uncomfortable?" I asked.

She put her free hand on my shoulder. "Not at all." Her eyes bored into mine. "I'm not as naive as you think, Rip. Inexperienced, yes. Unaware of what happens between a man and a woman, no."

At this moment, she sounded more like Maeve than herself. I took a breath and opened my mouth to speak, but Pearl beat me to it.

"What I'm feeling isn't because you rescued me. Nor is it because I see you as my savior. If anything, those two things should make me feel the opposite way I do."

I inhaled the scent of her, realizing again how much I'd missed seeing her, first thing this morning. "Why is that?"

"If I did, I'd probably see you the same way as Mr. Robinson or even my father. Instead, I see you as the only man who's made me feel things I never wanted to before."

When I leaned forward, just slightly, Pearl did too. It was impossible to say which of us initiated our first kiss. There was no question about who deepened it. She did, and I let her, emitting a soft groan from somewhere deep inside me and reveling in both her aggression and the taste of blueberry pancakes on her tongue.

As much as I wanted to move my hand from her waist, grip her ass, and align her body with mine, I forced myself to stay put and pressed my fingers into the flesh of her waist instead.

"Maeve said to let you know the pancakes are ready," I heard Hammer say at the same time Pearl broke our kiss and took a step back.

"We'll be right in," I said without looking away from her.

"Oh, and the plane is ready whenever you are."

"Roger that."

Hammer cleared his throat, but I ignored him. However, when Pearl looked increasingly uncomfortable, I asked him to give us a minute.

"We're being rude," she said when we heard the sliding door close.

"He's being nosy." As I said the words, I touched the tip of her nose with mine. "We're leaving for Colorado today. It's very cold there right now, so we'll need to get you a winter jacket of some kind before we go. Everything else you need can wait until we arrive."

"Will there be snow?"

"Yes, and a great deal of it."

Pearl's eyes lit up.

"Believe me, when you have to shovel the stuff, the excitement of seeing it wears off quick."

"I've never seen more than a dusting."

"From what I've heard on the weather reports, you're going to see several feet of it."

"I can help shovel."

I shook my head. "I'd lose my membership in the cowboy club if anyone at the Roaring Fork saw you." I dropped my arm from around her waist. "Come on, let's eat so we can be on our way."

When we walked in the door that led from the patio into the kitchen, Maeve was smiling.

"I think I've mastered the pancake flip," she said, holding out a plate in Pearl's direction.

"It looks perfect," she told her.

"And tastes even better," Hammer added between forkfuls.

"I'll make you a plate," Pearl offered.

"I can do it. Have a seat."

She nudged me. "I want to."

I held up both hands. "Okay, have at it."

I sat next to Hammer at the small dining table. "Who's piloting?" I asked.

"I didn't ask. Last time I did, I hadn't heard of either the captain or the co-pilot."

I smiled. "Copy that. Just so you know, I talked to Buck earlier, and we're good to stay at the ranch for as long as we need to."

Hammer nodded between more mouthfuls of pancakes. I dug in with equal fervor when Pearl set a plate in front of me. She went back into the kitchen, but returned seconds later with a cup of coffee. After setting that down too, she pulled out the chair beside me.

"Tell me about where we're staying," she said, taking a sip of her own coffee.

I wiped my mouth with a napkin. "It's a ranch much like this one—"

"Only quadruple the size," said Hammer.

I chuckled. "I think it's more than that."

"Whatever you do, don't ask," Maeve said from the kitchen. "Evidently, asking men the size of things is considered rude."

Hammer laughed and shook his head. "I'll never hear the end of that."

Pearl looked at me with scrunched eyes.

"Some men feel inadequate if the size of their… ranch…is smaller than that of another man."

Pearl laughed too. "I'll have to remember to never ask."

As I polished off the first stack and returned for seconds, I thought about the normalcy of the scene. Two couples, sharing breakfast and conversation. Inside jokes between each of them. Laughter. Smiling. Warmth. I loved the feeling of it.

I'd predict it would be the same when we were in Colorado. Buck had three brothers and a sister. He and his sister were the only two currently married.

"Irish and Flynn had a baby too, right?" I asked Hammer when Pearl got up and took our plates to the sink. "Leave those, and I'll clean up the kitchen in a minute," I called after her.

"Two. Twin boys."

"Do you know when?"

Hammer studied me. "No clue, but my guess is maybe six months ago. Why?"

"Isn't that something we should know?"

Hammer shrugged. "I guess. I'm sure somebody keeps track of it."

"What do you mean?"

"Decker or somebody."

"Decker Ashford?" I laughed.

Hammer shrugged again. "Yeah, seems unlikely."

"Unless he developed some kind of technology that does it for him."

Hammer looked around the kitchen. "Where did Maeve go?"

"No idea." I didn't see Pearl either.

"There's a reason women make such good agents."

"Yeah? How's that?"

"First of all, they can keep even the most mundane of secrets as though the fate of the world depends on it. Second, sometimes it's like they disappear into thin air. I didn't hear either of them leave."

I couldn't even recall if Pearl responded when I told her I'd clean up the dishes. "Maybe we should look for them."

Hammer leaned in close to me. "Before we do that, are you sure you know what you're doing with Pearl?"

"It was a kiss. That's it."

"Like that's never led to more."

"I plan to take it very slow with her," I assured him.

"That should be easy with the two of you stayin' in the same cabin."

While I wondered if it might be a good idea to bring a female operative in on Pearl's detail, the thought that hers wouldn't be the first face I saw when I got up and made my way into the kitchen in the morning left me feeling unsettled. I also wasn't sure I could handle not knowing that she was safe. And that meant twenty-four seven.

"I care about her, Hammer. A lot. I know it seems crazy since I only met her a few days ago, but the amount of time doesn't change how I feel."

He continued to study me but sat back in his chair. "That's something I can identify with."

He didn't have to tell me. I'd watched it happen between Maeve and him. I noticed their mutual attraction as early as her first day here on the ranch.

"I'll brief Money and Vex today about us leaving."

"Copy that. Have you given any more thought to a DNA test?"

"It's a good idea, but I want to discuss it with Pearl first."

"Maybe we should try to find her and Maeve," Hammer suggested, pushing out his chair and standing.

When I did the same, I was happy to see the dishes were still in the kitchen. "You find them; I'll clean up."

I'd just finished drying the griddle when he returned with both women. "Maeve was giving Pearl clothes to take to Colorado."

"Thanks," I said to Hammer's wife. "I figured we'd need to get a jacket, but we could get the rest once we landed in Gunnison."

"Saves you the trip, and I can't fit into any of it anyway."

Pearl thanked her for at least the second time, probably more, given Maeve laughed and rolled her eyes at the same time she said, *"You're welcome, again."*

"We should be on our way. Don't want to keep the pilots and plane tied up."

Maeve and Pearl hugged as though they were long-lost friends who would never see each other again. Hammer shook my hand and patted my back.

"Let me know if there's anything I can do to help," he said when the two walked us out to my SUV.

"How are you doing?" I asked Pearl once we were inside and I'd started the engine.

"Nervous. I've never been on an airplane before. Maeve told me there really wasn't anything to it but said sometimes it gets bumpy."

On the drive back to my place, I explained turbulence, but not in great detail. I'd never had a smooth ride into any of the Colorado airports, so I was glad Maeve thought to mention it.

"You're going to love the Roaring Fork." I told her a little bit about the place and how the family all lived on the ranch.

When I explained about the dining hall and how the Wheaton family also ran a dude ranch on the property, Pearl got a funny look on her face.

"What?" I asked.

"It sounds like the compound."

I had to admit it did. "Without rules, though." I laughed, thinking about what Buck's wife, Stella, would do if anyone tried to impose a single rule on her or any other women on the ranch. I had a feeling Flynn would react in a similar way.

"There must be some rules."

I shrugged. "Other than not doing anything considered illegal and being respectful of one another, I can't think of one. Using the security in place. All of those things are a given rather than a rule per se."

An hour later, Crash, someone I knew well from several different missions, greeted us when we boarded the Invincibles' private jet.

"Who's flying with you today?" I asked.

"Angel and I fly together almost exclusively."

Crash had been a fighter pilot with the Air Force, and Angel the same but with the British equivalent. I'd also heard a rumor the two were romantically involved.

The door to the lavatory opened seconds later, and Angel came out. I introduced both to Pearl.

"Skies are clear and quiet today. I expect we'll land at the Gunnison airport somewhere around two hours after we get into the air," Angel said before turning to Pearl. "I hear this is your first flight."

When the two women went into the cockpit, Crash and I walked toward the plane's aft. "Have you been read in on this mission?" I asked.

"Only that it involves asset protection and the ABT are the bad guys."

"That's pretty much all you need to know."

I waited until Pearl joined me before taking a seat. She appeared in awe. I had to admit I was, too, the first few times I flew somewhere on this jet.

"Do you want to sit near a window?" I asked.

"I don't think so."

I chose two seats and helped Pearl get her seat belt fastened. As I did, something else occurred to me. "Have you ever had alcohol? You know, like a beer or wine?"

She shook her head. "It wasn't permitted. What about you?"

"I like beer from time to time. Otherwise, I steer clear of the harder stuff."

"My father liked the harder stuff, as you called it."

"What happened when he drank?" I asked.

"He'd get angry. He never took it out on me, but I also did my best to keep out of his way if I knew he'd had a couple. That's what he'd call it."

"Pearl, how much do you know about your father's background?"

"Nothing. I mean, I know he's been in prison but has been out for a long time. Since I was born almost."

"He never mentioned your mother?"

She shook her head. "And I knew better than to ask."

"What would've happened if you had?"

"I never wanted to find out."

It was a shitty fucking way to live. Not being able to ask about your own mother. "No one on the compound ever said anything either?"

"None of the women ever brought it up, and most of the men never spoke to me at all."

"I'm sorry you experienced that way of life. I told you before, you can ask me whatever you want to.

If there is a reason I can't answer you outright, I'll explain why not."

She looked beyond me, seemingly out the window, when the plane started to move. "Maeve said I should ask you to hold my hand."

"That's not something you ever have to ask for, Pearl. You want to hold my hand, go right ahead. I'll never mind."

14

Pearl

Maeve was probably the most straightforward woman I'd ever met. Even more so than Ms. Shay. I appreciated her telling me I'd be frightened when the plane took off and landed but, once we were in the air, I wouldn't even realize we were moving.

She'd been right about takeoff. I squeezed Rip's hand so hard he winced. He didn't let go, though. When the plane seemed to level off and he asked if I wanted to switch seats so I could look out the window, I took him up on the offer.

There were so many things I wanted to ask him. Where he'd grown up and what his parents were like, since he'd asked me about mine. I also wanted to know things that pertained more to me. Specifically, what would eventually happen or where I'd go. However, I was so mesmerized by the clouds beneath us that I couldn't tear myself away from watching them. Whenever I did, just to look over my shoulder at Rip, he'd smile.

All of a sudden, something dawned on me. I couldn't believe I'd forgotten Mojo. In fact, I didn't even remember seeing my stuffed bear. I tried really hard not to cry when I turned to look at Rip again.

"What's wrong?" he asked.

"Mojo."

Like before, he smiled.

"I know you think it's funny, but—"

He held up one finger, unfastened his seat belt, and went toward the front of the plane. He got out his suitcase, opened it just a little, and pulled Mojo from inside.

"Why didn't you say something?" I asked when he handed him to me.

He shrugged. "Can't help it. I like being the hero. If you'd have asked earlier, I would've. Then I forgot."

I hugged my teddy bear close to me. "Thank you so much. I know it seems—"

"I'm sorry to interrupt, but please don't say it seems silly, or anything else like that. I think it's sweet, and honestly, it doesn't surprise or bother me. You were taken from everything you knew, Pearl. What does surprise me is how okay you seem."

"That's because I'm with you. If I weren't, I'm not sure I'd be okay at all."

"You're more resilient than you think."

"It's only because of people like you and Maeve. Hammer too. And Mr. Robinson and Ms. Shay, of course." Since we were already talking about it, I figured I should probably continue. "What's going to happen to me?"

"Before I respond, there's something I'd like to talk to you about."

I didn't like the look on Rip's face one bit. He was no longer smiling, and worse, he appeared troubled.

"Go ahead."

"Ms. Shay, as you call her, told you she believed you were in danger."

"That's right. As did you."

"However, she wasn't specific about what that danger was. Is that right?"

"Neither were you."

"We never finished the conversation we began about who I really am—who they really are—but more importantly, why you're in danger."

"You're scaring me."

"Ms. Shay overheard someone in the ABT say he believed you might be of value to the Aryan Nation. Do you know who Luke Howell is?"

"The name doesn't sound familiar."

"Did your father ever say anything about a connection to the ABT's parent organization?"

"He did not."

"Pearl, there's reason to believe your dad wasn't actually your biological father."

I clutched Mojo tighter to me as I let his words sink in. I definitely looked nothing like him, but I figured I must favor my mother. Not that I'd seen any photos of her to indicate one way or another. But my dad, or whoever he was, had always treated me well—like a daughter.

"I don't understand."

"Since you've never had a reason to need identification, it would be easy to conceal your identity."

"Why would he?"

"It's a very good question. I believe the answer is the reason you're in danger."

"What does this have to do with me asking what will happen to me?"

"I'd like it if you got a DNA test. It can confirm whether John Fischer was or wasn't biologically related to you. There's also a chance we'll find your actual birth parents. Or at least one of them."

"How?"

Rip explained that many people were getting the same kind of tests he thought I should have and it was leading to some finding siblings or other relatives they never knew they had.

"It would mean someone related to me would have to have the test too."

"That's right."

"Rip, what else aren't you telling me?" He got a certain look in his eyes when he was holding something back.

"When someone is arrested for a felony, they're automatically tested, and those records remain in the criminal justice system."

"Meaning you think if my father wasn't…my father, whoever really was, was in prison too."

"It's one possibility. Another is that you were kidnapped and brought to the compound. If that was the case, it's likely your birth parents underwent testing, just with the hope they'd find you."

"Does it hurt?" I asked.

"Not at all. They do what's called a swab, where they put a stick with cotton on it into your mouth and run it over the inside of your cheek."

"Do they do that for other tests?"

"Maybe. I'm not sure. Why do you ask?"

"Because someone did that to me not long after my dad died."

"Who?"

"A man in the infirmary."

"Someone you didn't know?" Rip asked.

"That's right."

He pulled out his phone and tapped several things on the screen before setting it on the small table between us. "I asked for a photo of Luke Howell."

"To see if he was the one who did the test?"

Rip nodded. A few minutes later, it vibrated. "Is this him?" he asked, holding his phone so I could see it.

"Yes."

"Who did he say he was?"

"He didn't."

"He also didn't explain what he was doing. Is that right?"

"Men on the compound don't have to explain anything to the women. If a woman persists in asking questions, it's considered a reason for her to receive a punishment."

"Understood."

We were both quiet for some time. I'd even lost interest in looking out the window at the clouds. What if I did this and found out I had different parents? Or that I'd been kidnapped?

That part didn't make any sense, though. I was a grown woman, an adult. If I wasn't really my father's daughter, why would he have kept me with him once I was of age? The other thing was, if I wasn't his daughter, why hadn't he claimed me himself? No one on the compound would've said a word to him about it. That kind of thing happened in some of the families.

Rip put his hand on mine. "I didn't answer your first question, did I? What will happen to you."

I nodded, not wanting to know anymore. I wasn't sure I'd really wanted to know in the first place.

"I will take care of you, make sure you're safe, for as long as you need or want me to. No matter what information the DNA test comes back with, I won't force you to go be or live with anyone who makes you uncomfortable. That includes me, Pearl. If you're uncomfortable with me, we can assign someone else to your detail."

My detail? What did that mean? "Like who?"

"Another woman, for example. Someone like Ms. Shay."

"I don't want that." Ms. Shay had always been kind to me. That wasn't the issue. I didn't like the idea of being away from Rip. Even when I left earlier and walked to Hammer and Maeve's house, there were several times I thought about turning around and going back. Part of me was afraid of this very thing. That he'd ask someone else to let me stay with them.

"If you change your mind, all you have to do is say so."

"What about you?"

His head cocked. "What about me?"

"Do you want me to stay with someone else?"

Rip looked me in the eye but didn't speak for what felt like an hour but was probably only seconds. "There isn't anything I want less than that. I already told you I will take care of you and make sure you're safe for as long as you want me to."

"What if it was forever?" I whispered.

"Then, it would be forever."

15

Rip

Pearl might not believe me, but I meant it. I'd never, ever turn my back on her. In fact, I would've been disappointed if she'd said she wanted a female to take over her detail. I'd breathed a silent sigh of relief when she said she didn't.

"We'll be landing soon," Crash said when he opened the door of the cockpit and stuck his head out. "You have at least twenty minutes before we do, but I wanted to give you fair warning."

"What do we need to do?" Pearl asked.

"Hold hands."

She looked at me and smiled. "Thank you, Rip."

I brought the hand she'd covered mine with to my mouth and kissed the back of it. "You're welcome."

"What were your parents like?" she asked.

"They still live in Wyoming, where I grew up."

"Why don't you live there?"

I'd anticipated her question and wanted to give her the most honest answer I could. "My dad and I never saw eye to eye. Mainly because we're too much alike."

"What about your mother?"

"She had to play referee when I was growing up. I try hard not to put her in that position anymore. Part of that involves keeping my distance."

"When's the last time you saw them?"

It had been too long, and that had definitely been on my mind. "It's been more than a year. I'm due for a visit soon."

"I bet I'd like them."

Her statement surprised me. "What makes you say that?"

"I like you. They raised you. I bet I'd like your dad a lot if the two of you have so much in common."

There were times Pearl's simple way of thinking was so childlike. Then others, her maturity surprised me. "I like you too."

"Tell me about your mother."

I smiled. She was as good as they came. Down-to-earth, hardworking, and believed in treating others the way she wanted to be treated. I doubted there was ever anyone who had a bad word to say about the woman.

"She likes to cook, but not bake as much as my nana did. She also crochets and knits. I can never remember the difference between the two, although she always says they are nothing alike."

"What does she make?"

"Cooking or the other stuff?"

"Both."

"As far as the other stuff, she makes blankets and booties for babies. I'm pretty sure everyone born in Cheyenne in the last twenty years had them. Maybe longer than that." It made me realize those would've made really nice gifts for my friends who'd recently had kids of their own. While I hadn't thought of it before, I should ask her for something for a baby girl for Hammer and Maeve's daughter. It was probably too late to give anything to Buck and Stella or Irish and Flynn.

"What are you thinking about?" Pearl asked.

"You'll laugh."

"Maybe, but I still want to know."

I told her my idea about getting something from my mom for Maeve and Hammer's daughter.

"Did you know she'll have the same name as Maeve and Maeve's mom and grandmother and great-grandmother and even her mother? I think that's so cool."

I felt the plane's descent at the same time Pearl did. She clutched my hand tighter.

"Sorry. I'll try not to hurt you this time."

"Takes a lot more than you squeezing my hand a little to hurt me, darlin'."

"What do I have to do to get that test done?" she asked.

Her abrupt change of subject surprised me. "Tell me you're okay with doing it."

"I'm okay."

"I'll get it arranged."

She nodded, but I could see the worry etched on her face. John Fischer might not have been the greatest man there ever was nor the most law-abiding one, but from the sound of it, he treated Pearl okay. The old saying of better a fool you know than a devil you don't was certainly true in this case. God knew who Pearl's biological parents might be. Whoever it was had to have something to do with the Aryan Nation if Luke Howell figured out he should test her DNA.

An SUV similar to mine was parked on the tarmac near where Crash maneuvered the plane. "Your chariot awaits," he said from the cockpit when Pearl and I were about to deplane.

"What about the two of you?" I asked.

"Headed back to Texas in under an hour."

"I hope I didn't delay someone else's plans."

"Not at all. That's pretty much our base now."

"Well, damn, I didn't know that. We should get together sometime."

Crash and Angel both said they'd like to, even though at this point, I had no idea when it might be.

Pearl thanked them, and we walked down the stairs that had been wheeled over to the plane. When we reached the bottom, Buck got out of the waiting vehicle.

"Welcome home," he said, rushing over to help with our bags.

I shook my head and laughed. "Texas has been my home for quite some time now."

"Yeah, but Colorado holds a special place in your heart. Admit it."

The funny part was, until recently, after his father passed away, Buck had vowed never to live in the state again. Now, he and Stella were settled on the Roaring

Fork, and from what I'd heard, had no plans to live anywhere else.

"I'm Buck," he said, holding his hand out to Pearl, who introduced herself.

"Stella stayed at the house with Buckaroo, but I told her I'd be sure to invite you over as soon as you're settled."

It typically took thirty minutes to drive from the airport in Gunnison to the ranch's gates in Crested Butte, but today would be longer, mainly because of the traffic on the two-lane road.

"Damn tourists," Buck muttered a couple of times on the way. "It's ski season," he eventually explained to Pearl. "People come from all over the world to ski here, but some of them have either never driven in the snow or it's been a long time since they last did, so they have no idea how to do it."

"I don't know how to drive at all," she admitted.

"No better place than the ranch if you want to learn. We'll even make sure whatever vehicle Rip gets to drive around in is an automatic."

"Automatic what?" she looked over the seat to me and asked.

"Transmission," I answered. "Most cars aren't made with standard ones anymore anyway, so don't worry about it. It's just that some of the Roaring Fork trucks are older than I am."

Pearl's eyes opened wide, but she had a huge smile on her face. I couldn't wait until we arrived and I could ask her what had made her so happy. Maybe it was Buck saying she could learn to drive while we were here if she wanted to. While he hadn't said those exact words, it was clearly implied.

"Wow," she exclaimed when we rounded a bend and Mount Crested Butte came into view. "That's amazing."

"She's a beauty," I mumbled.

"Do you ski?" she asked.

"Him or me?" said Buck.

"Both of you."

"We do. If you could call it that."

"What does that mean?"

Buck laughed. "Neither of us was ever very good at it."

"Hey, speak for yourself," I grumbled. "I was better than you were."

This time, Buck roared with laughter. "Not even close, man. Not even close. My brothers, on the other hand, are good skiers. Snowboarders too."

"What about your sister?"

"She didn't do too much of it," Buck answered.

"Why not?"

The truth was she hadn't been allowed to. Buck's father was a first-class asshole, and not just because he didn't want his daughter out, skiing. I hated that Buck was on the spot right now, but I was anxious to hear how he'd respond.

"Never interested her too much." He looked away when he said it. I knew he was lying and figured Pearl did too.

We only suffered a few more minutes of awkward silence before Buck pulled up to the ranch gate and waited for it to open. "Welcome to the Roaring Fork."

"It's beautiful," she said with evident awe.

"Sure is," I added.

Buck drove to the front of the old farmhouse just inside the gate. They'd done a lot more work to it since the last time I saw it. "I know I said I'd invite you over once you were settled, but Stella really wants to see Rip and meet you, Pearl. Mind if we stop in and say hello?"

"I was hoping we would," I told him, climbing out and opening Pearl's door for her. "Stella, Buck's wife, is great. You're going to love her."

"I don't doubt it. Every person you introduce me to is nicer than the one before. I don't mean that literally," she stammered. "Just that everyone is so nice."

I put my arm around her shoulders. "I knew what you meant, darlin'."

I caught Buck's raised eyebrows. First Hammer, now him. I suppose it was to be expected.

Not that I was surprised, but Pearl and Stella got on just as well as she had with Maeve. We weren't there long before she was holding the baby.

"Got a minute?" Buck asked. Seeing how comfortable Pearl appeared, I followed him out the front door to the porch.

"Before you comment, Pearl and I are…close."

Buck raised both hands like I so often did. Maybe that's where I'd gotten it from. "Wasn't going to say a word."

"What did you need to discuss with me?"

"I wanted to give you an update on what's happening here at the ranch. Porter hasn't been here much in the last few months."

"No?" That surprised me. Porter had been the one who was adamant about the ranch getting into raising roughstock.

"More of my father's bullshit."

I nodded in understanding. Back when Roscoe B. Wheaton died, Buck and his siblings were called into the attorney's office for what they believed would be a standard reading of the will. Instead, they found out the old man had put a stipulation in, stating that in order for any of the siblings to inherit the land or a penny of the money in the estate, Buck had to live on the property full-time for a solid year. Given he did what I did for a living, that was no easy feat, but he'd managed it.

As much as it likely rankled Buck, his father was probably looking down—or up if you asked him or his siblings—patting himself on the back for bringing his eldest son back into the family fold. Especially since Buck and Stella now considered it home and were so happy, living on the ranch.

"What's Porter's penance?"

Buck laughed. "You sure used the right word for it."

When he didn't answer my question, I didn't ask a second time.

"Anyway, he isn't here, and I'm not sure when he'll be back."

"Copy that. What about Holt and Cord?"

"Holt is still traveling with CB Rice. Cord is a full-time wrangler with the dude ranch."

CB Rice, the band Buck mentioned, was one of my favorites. "They playin' around here anywhere?"

"I think they're fixin' to put on a show here, at the Roaring Fork, as a matter of fact."

"I'll look forward to it. Anything else you want me to know?"

"Flynn and Irish are happy as could be. Their two boys are growin' like you wouldn't believe."

What I couldn't believe was what I was about to ask. "What are their names?"

"Paxon and Rooker."

I knew Paxon was named after Irish, the twins' father. "Rooker?"

"It was my mama's maiden name. We call 'em Pax and Rook."

"From the sound of things, your family is in a good place."

Buck looked out at the horizon. "Everybody but Porter."

"You feel like talkin' about it?"

"Not my story to tell."

"Copy that. If you talk to him, let him know I said hello."

When Buck and I went inside, Pearl and Stella were laughing hard at something.

"What's so funny?" Buck asked.

"Pearl wanted to know what TJ stood for."

I knew the story well. Stella—a nickname given to her by another agent Buck and I worked with—had been called TJ when she was growing up. She was one of the world's most hard-hitting investigative reporters. Not just tough as nails. More like railroad spikes. When she finally admitted what the acronym stood for, everyone who knew her understood why she'd kept it a secret. *Tiffany Joy*—and there wasn't a less fitting name for anyone.

"You probably want to be on your way and get settled," Stella said, taking the baby from Pearl's arms. "But don't be a stranger. You can come over and visit this little guy and me whenever you want." She looked up at her husband. "Oh, and the big guy too, although I have a feeling he'll be spending as much time as he can with Rip. He missed you, my friend."

"And I missed the both of you," I responded sincerely. I hadn't realized how much until we arrived here.

"I put you in the biggest North Fork cabin," Buck said after we'd left the farmhouse. "It's the one Stella and I first stayed in." He wriggled his eyebrows, and I laughed.

"I remember."

Pearl looked between us.

"You don't wanna know," I said.

"Come on, it isn't that bad." Buck laughed.

"In this case, bad and boring are interchangeable."

"I'm gonna tell Stella you said that." We both laughed at that.

"I like how you are with your friends," Pearl said after we'd each taken some time to get ourselves unpacked in rooms that were across the hall from one another. Like Stella had been back before she and Buck were together, I put Pearl in the bigger of the two, the one that had an en-suite bathroom.

"They're a lot of fun. As you saw."

"I envy that," she said when we went out to the kitchen and I opened the fridge to see if Flynn, who ran the catering side of the dude ranch, had stocked it with food. I wasn't disappointed.

"Hungry?" I asked, pulling containers out whether she was or not. It had been too long since I'd had Roaring Fork BBQ, and couldn't wait to dig in.

"Starving, actually." Pearl joined me, opening container after container. "What is all this?" she asked.

"Flynn's specialties—BBQ pork, tri-tip, potato salad, macaroni salad, mac and cheese, and coleslaw. Damn, I missed this food."

While we heated up the pork and beef, I piled our plates with the sides. "Anything you don't want?"

"I want some of each, please," she said, watching me get the containers of meat from the microwave while she set the small kitchen table.

"About what you said. You know, envying my relationship with my friends. You're already establishing some of your own, Pearl. Maeve adores you, and it looked like Stella did, too. I'm sure Scottie feels the same way."

"Scottie?"

"Ms. Shay."

"Everyone is just so nice. I know I keep saying that, but it's true."

"I predict you and Flynn are going to hit it off too. That's Buck's sister."

"Stella told me about her. It sounds like she could use some help with the two baby boys."

I set Pearl's plate on the table and held out her chair for her to be seated.

"Thank you, sir," she said. "I mean—"

"It's okay. I'm sorry I made you self-conscious about that."

Pearl nodded. "Thank you," she repeated.

We were both quiet while we ate, but when Pearl asked if I was finished and got up to take our plates to the sink, I asked her to sit back down.

"What's wrong?"

"Nothing. I just want to be sure you understand that no one expects you to 'earn your keep' while you're here. Anywhere else, for that matter."

Making her pout was the last thing I'd meant to do, but it's sure what I did. "I like being useful."

"I know you do. What I'm saying is that you don't *have* to."

"Okay, so *may* I help Flynn?"

"That's the other thing. You don't have to ask my permission."

Pearl put her elbows on the table and her head in her hands.

"What's wrong?" I asked this time.

"It's all so confusing. While living on the compound was difficult, at least I knew what I was supposed to do and when I was supposed to do it. All of this is just so…complicated."

Her words reminded me of things I'd read about why some women preferred living in a cult environment.

"Would it help if we talked about our days? Maybe every morning, you can tell me what you want to do, and I can tell you what I have planned."

"I'd like that, but you still haven't answered me about whether I can help Flynn. If she even wants my help."

"If that's what you want to do, of course you can. By the way, Buck said a band his brother Holt is in might be playing a show here on the ranch. Is that something you'd like to see?"

When she nodded and her eyes lit up, relief washed over me.

She looked out the window. "I'll miss our rides."

"We can still ride out if you want. I plan to."

"Even in the snow?"

"You just have to dress for it." Actually, that gave me another idea. "Be right back," I told her, going to grab my phone.

16

Pearl

"Are we going for a ride now?" I asked when Rip came back and told me to put on the warmest clothes I'd brought with me.

"Not exactly, but we will be outside for a bit."

I stood where I was, unsure what to do next. I mean, I knew I was supposed to change, but it would've been so much easier if I knew what we were doing.

"I'm sorry. I've done it again, haven't I?"

"Done what?"

"Not told you what you need to know."

I hung my head. "I'm just not used to…surprises." That had become especially true after my father died. Every minute of every day had been regimented unless I was with Mr. Robinson and Ms. Shay.

"When I went into the bedroom earlier, I called one of Buck's brothers to see if there would be a sleigh ride tonight. He said since there were no guests on the ranch other than us, he hadn't planned one. I asked if he could…as a surprise."

"A sleigh ride?"

"You know, like Santa."

I knew "who" Santa was. Or what. Not that we'd ever celebrated Christmas on the compound. We read about Jesus in our studies, but that didn't mean we made a big deal about his birth. I'd heard some of the other women talking about how they missed it.

I'd turned my head away, and when I looked back, Rip was standing right in front of me.

"I'm going to work harder to understand the way your life has been, Pearl. I'm sorry if I keep getting carried away. I just find myself wanting to spoil you. Do you know what that means?"

"The other women on the compound would tell you I'm already plenty spoiled."

He shook his head. "Not even a little. If you don't want to go on a sleigh ride, we don't have to."

"I do, though."

"Tell you what. Afterwards, we'll sit by the fire, and you can tell me more about your days when you were living on the compound. Then we can meet somewhere in the middle, like we did at the Hammered Dubliner."

I had been comfortable there. It was easy to see the kinds of things I could do to help out at Rip's house. Even though I hadn't had time to work for Hammer and Maeve, I still understood what would be expected of me. I couldn't just sit around all day and do nothing. I'd go crazy. Like Rip said, we could meet in the middle. I'd know what I could be doing, and he wouldn't feel like he was pushing me too hard.

"Thank you," I said when I realized he was waiting for a response.

"You sure you still want to go? I can call Cord and tell him we changed our minds."

"I'd like to."

Rip looked so happy; I felt bad for taking his excitement away a few minutes ago. I wished I knew how to be "less regimented," but I'd never had the opportunity to learn how to be. Even this morning, when I got up and took off on foot to talk to Maeve, my original plan was to tell her I was there to work. She'd immediately known that wasn't the case, though.

Maybe part of our "meeting in the middle" was that I'd work harder to understand the kinds of things that made Rip happy. He loved spending time with his friends. Riding out too. It was his favorite thing to do.

While I couldn't imagine going for a ride with as cold as it was here, or picture the horses trudging through the snow, next time he mentioned it, I'd agree to go along willingly.

"Willingly" wasn't a word I was accustomed to using. Happily wasn't, either. I was used to doing what I was told. No one cared if I was willing or happy about it. If I'd ever argued, it would've gotten me another whipping at the hitching post. I cringed at the memory.

"What's on your mind, Pearl?"

I looked up from my wringing fingers, not even realizing I was doing it. "Bad memories."

He reached out and took my hands in his. "Let's make some good ones—you and me."

The sleigh ride we took last night turned out to be one of the funnest, sweetest, most romantic things I'd ever experienced. I'd dressed warmly, like Rip told me to, but still covered up with the warm blankets that were on the sleigh when I came out of the cabin.

Rip was an expert driver and maneuvered the two horses that pulled us all around the ranch. We went by the main house, which is where he said Flynn and her husband lived. He also took me to see some of the other cabins he said he'd helped build.

Later this morning, we'd be going to the hospital, which Rip said was near the airport where we flew in, to get my DNA test. Now that I knew that was what the man had done at the compound's infirmary, I wasn't afraid. I couldn't help but worry about what the results would tell us, though.

I still couldn't believe John Fischer wasn't my father. Sometimes, I hoped the test would prove he was. Other times, I thought about the possibility that my mother was somewhere out in the world, and when I found her, she'd be so happy to see me she wouldn't be able to stop hugging me.

There was the chance, too, that whoever my real parents were, were worse people than John Fischer had been. I didn't like to think about that possibility.

I was just about to make a cup of coffee when I heard a door open. I raised my head in time to see Rip come out of the bedroom and go into the bathroom. He was dressed just like he had been that first morning I woke up in his house—just with a pair of jeans. No shirt, no boots. Instead of drinking the coffee myself, I walked over to the hall and waited for him.

"Here you go," I said, handing him the cup when he came out.

"Thanks." He took it with one hand and reached up to smooth his hair with the other. Before I could talk myself out of it, I trailed one finger from his neck all the way down his body to his belly button. When Rip shuddered under my touch, I felt empowered enough to keep going until I reached the top button of his jeans that he'd left open. Only then did he lower his arm and stop me from going farther.

"You have a nice body," I murmured. "It makes me want to run my fingers all over it."

Rip's breath hitched. I smiled and raised my other hand, resting it on his chest. He bent over and set his coffee on the floor. When he stood upright, he wrapped his arms around my waist and brought his forehead to mine. "I want to run my fingers all over your body too, Pearl," he said, his voice thicker, heavier than I'd heard it before. "Not just my fingers."

"What else?" I whispered.

"My lips. My tongue."

I shuddered like he had, squeezing my legs together when my body started to tingle between them. Rather than wait for him to kiss me, I touched my lips to his.

When I did, Rip raised one hand, gripped the back of my neck, and used his tongue to press my mouth open. His kiss was soft and gentle, caressing my tongue with his, angling his head to tighten his mouth's hold on mine. His intensity stole every thought from my mind other than getting as close to him as I possibly could.

When I brought my pelvis to his, Rip moved one hand to my bottom and held me still. I was dizzy with feelings I didn't understand, let alone recognize. I *wanted* but didn't know what exactly. My nipples throbbed as though the only thing that could soothe them was his mouth. I didn't want to let it go, though. Every sweep of his tongue felt like a gift. Rip gave and gave; he didn't take.

I snaked my hand between our two bodies and rested my fingers where they were before, when he'd stopped me. I could feel his coarse hair and how much tighter his jeans had gotten. What would he do if I unfastened all the buttons? Would he stop me, or would he let me touch his hardness?

Before I could, a knock on the cabin's door startled us both. "That'll be Flynn," he said, releasing his hold on me and taking a step back. "You get the door, and I'll go put more clothes on."

I groaned in frustration, but when I peeked over my shoulder, I could see the woman standing on the other side of the door as well as she could see me. I was about to rush over to let her in, but Rip grabbed my wrist.

"Wait. I need one more kiss."

It was quick, but it made me giggle.

"Hi, you must be Pearl," the woman said when I opened the door. "I'm Flynn, and I'm so sorry to… interrupt." Her cheeks flushed in the same way I knew mine were. "I just wanted to stop by and say hi to Rip, and meet you, of course. Oh, and I brought you this." She held out a basket, and I took the handle.

"Do you want to come in? Rip will just be a minute."

"If you wouldn't mind. It's been so long since I've seen him. You know, he's practically like a brother to me. Gah, I'm running at the mouth, aren't I? I'm so sorry. You must think I'm absolutely crazy. It's the lack of sleep, I tell ya. Twin boys, ya know? Maybe you don't know. Sorry. Again. I have twin boys. Babies. As soon as I get one to sleep, the other wakes up—"

"Flynn Wheaton, are you ever a sight. Look at you! You're beaming." Rip came out of the bedroom, hurried over, and hugged the woman.

"I've never been happier."

Rip laughed. "I can tell. You haven't stopped talking long enough to take a breath since Pearl opened the door."

I thought maybe Flynn would take offense to what he'd said, but she didn't seem to. Instead, she laughed like he had. "He knows me too well. When I'm happy, I jabber on like an idiot."

"And when she's unhappy, good luck getting a word out of her." The look on Rip's face was so sweet. It was obvious this woman meant a lot to him. I wasn't jealous, though. It felt brotherly.

"I was just about to make coffee," I said. "Would you like a cup?"

"I'd love a decaf, but make yours first. I can unpack your breakfast." Flynn took the basket from my hand and set it on the dining table. "Did you find the food I left for you last night?"

"Did you make all that?" I gasped. "It was so delicious. Every bite."

Flynn's cheeks flushed. "My brother Cord smokes the meat, but the other stuff is mine." She opened the fridge and looked inside. "I guess you did like it. The containers look nearly empty."

"Go sit. I'll handle this, and you and Pearl can get acquainted," said Rip, walking over and pulling her away from the refrigerator. "The only thing missing last night was some of your cornbread."

"I knew I forgot something. Darn it all. I'll drop some by later. Or you can come to the house and pick it up. You know, so I don't interrupt again."

"Go sit," Rip whispered.

I took my coffee over and sat beside the woman, who absolutely fascinated me as she continued rambling on, telling Rip about her babies and her husband, about the dude ranch, and her brothers.

"Did Buck tell you about Porter?" she asked him.

When Rip nodded, Flynn shook her head.

"My father was such an asshole," she muttered, then looked up at me. "Sorry for the language, but it's true."

"Did you bring us some muffins this mornin'?" Rip asked, moving the cloth napkin that covered the basket's contents.

"Oh goodness, I forgot to unpack your breakfast." When she reached over, Rip swatted her hand.

"I'll do it. I'm too hungry to wait for you." He winked, and she smiled.

"He's right. I'm hopeless. So, anyway, Pearl, welcome to Roaring Fork Ranch. You probably haven't had the chance to see much of it yet."

"We went on a sleigh ride last night," I told her. "It looked very beautiful by moonlight."

Flynn smiled. "That's right. Cord mentioned Rip wanted to take you out in the sleigh." She batted her eyelashes in his direction. "*So* romantic of you."

He shook his head and laughed.

"What's all this?" I asked when he took out several different types of muffins, some bread, and a glass jar that looked like it held jam.

"I'll get some plates," I offered, standing before he could tell me he'd do it. As I brushed past him and our eyes met, I wondered if he was thinking about earlier, as I was.

"We have an errand to run in Gunnison this morning, if there's anything you want us to pick up for you while we're there," Rip said once we were all seated at the table, eating.

Flynn took a bite of one of the muffins and looked up at the ceiling. "Nothing I can think of. Plus, Paxon and I sometimes take a drive there just to get the boys to fall asleep. Riding in the car does the trick every time.

Not just for them; I nod off too." She sighed. "My poor husband. Anyway, no, thanks. Why do you have to go to Gunnison?" She held up her hand in Rip's direction. "Never mind. Forget I asked. None of my business."

Once again, he shook his head and laughed.

"Speaking of the babies…" My eyes met Rip's, and he nodded. "I was wondering if you could maybe use some help while I'm here. I have lots of experience and—"

"Oh my God! Yes!" she blurted. "That would be amazing. Are you sure? Stella and I are pretty much the only women on the ranch. No offense to the guys or anything, but my babies just do better with women, I think. Well, except for their dad, of course. They absolutely adore him."

"Maybe we can swing by the house when we get back. I can get some of your cornbread, and Pearl can meet Irish and the twins."

"Who's Irish?" I asked.

"That was Paxon's code name." Flynn's hand came to her mouth. "I mean nickname."

"It's okay, darlin'," said Rip, rubbing her shoulder. "Pearl knows."

"Phew. I'm not very good at keeping all their secrets. I should be, since my brother used to work for the CIA. He wasn't around very much back then, though."

Flynn's cell phone rang, and she jumped up. "That'll be Paxon, wondering if I've gotten lost." She turned to me. "Not really. I mean, I wouldn't get lost on my own ranch. One of the twins—or both—is probably fussy. I best be on my way, but I'll see you both later?"

"You will," Rip responded.

I stood too. "Thank you for breakfast."

"You're so welcome. When you come by later, you can tell me what you'd like tomorrow." She waved behind her as she walked out the door. I closed it behind her and leaned against it.

"I'm *exhausted*."

Rip laughed out loud. "Yeah, Flynn is a lot to take in. Although she wasn't always the way she is now. I love seeing her so happy."

"How did she used to be?"

Rip held out his hand, I took it, and he pulled me into his arms. "Her father was, like she said, a bastard. Mean old *sonuvabitch*. Unfortunately, Flynn didn't escape his wrath."

My eyes opened wide. "Did he hurt her?"

"Not physically, that I know of anyway. His words did enough damage on their own, though."

"That's awful." I'd seen plenty of that on the compound. Men who were so mean, and their women were just expected to keep their mouths closed and take it. It was one of the reasons I'd never wanted one of them to claim me. I would've hated having to live that way.

"Sorry to say this, but we need to get on the road if we're going to get your test done today."

I nodded.

"You sure you're okay with doing this?" Rip asked.

"Better to just get it over with."

17

Rip

Flynn Wheaton—Warrick now—was the cold shower I needed after how intense things got between Pearl and me earlier.

While I didn't consider her cock-blocking arrival a good thing then, now I realized that if she hadn't shown up, nothing would've stopped me from ravishing the beautiful woman whose hands felt like heaven when she touched my body.

How in God's name I was going to keep our foray into intimacy from happening again was beyond me. Clearly, neither of us possessed enough control for abstinence. I could vow it now, but the minute she touched me again, I would be powerless to stop myself from reaching out for her too.

Now, though, we needed to get to Gunnison. Given a court order would help facilitate the expediency of the DNA test results, Hammer had made arrangements to get one on direct orders from the CIA. As far as the hospital was concerned, Pearl was bound by law to appear this morning to have the testing completed. There was still the matter of identification, but I had fake, illegal, and most importantly, *temporary* proof of her identity.

There were instances where Pearl could obtain legal documentation, but those took time. The alternate form had been put into place for the indigent or homeless and required proof of residency in a particular state. Typically, that proof could include a receipt for lodging or from a campground if receiving mail wasn't an option. Hammer had drawn up a letter to be mailed to Pearl here at the ranch, which meant when it arrived, we could work on getting her ID in the State of Colorado. Once we returned to Texas, we'd surrender it and obtain one from there.

"Ready?" I asked when she came out of the bedroom dressed in warm clothes and wearing a jacket and boots.

"Yes...Rip."

I stood in front of her and put my hands on her shoulders. "There isn't anything for you to be nervous about."

"I'm not. At least not about the test itself."

"But you are about the results. Look at it this way, John Fischer is dead. Whatever the test reveals, the time you spent as his daughter won't go away; it'll simply open up the potential for you to find your true parents. Whoever they are—good or bad—you'll know."

Pearl nodded but didn't say anything. She remained quiet on the way to the hospital and when we returned to the ranch after the test was complete.

"Do you want to stop by the main house and see Flynn?" I asked after we were through the ranch gates.

"Sure."

"Pearl, unless you tell me you *want* to stop in, we won't. I'm not forcing this. I'm helping you do what you said you wanted to do."

She looked at me for practically the first time since we left the house. "I'd rather not."

"Then, we won't."

I drove straight to the cabin, and after we arrived, Pearl went directly into the bedroom, saying she didn't feel well.

Her retreat into herself continued for the next three days. Pearl was polite but aloof to the point I worried about her.

CB Rice had played a few songs at the dining hall two nights ago, but when I suggested we go see them, she'd said she wasn't interested. I wasn't about to go without her.

Earlier on the day of the performance, I'd sent texts to both Buck and Flynn, updating them on Pearl's withdrawal and asking them to give us space. To Flynn, I added we had everything we needed at the cabin and if that changed, I'd let her know. Since she hadn't dropped by unannounced again, I assumed she read between the lines of my message. Since Pearl didn't ask about helping with the babies, I didn't bring it up either.

"The results should be in today," I said over breakfast—one of three times each day I saw her.

"Yes."

"Pearl—"

"Please don't."

"What? I was just going to say…"

She stood, took her dishes into the kitchen, and left them by the sink. I watched as she shuffled back to the bedroom and shut the door.

Before this abrupt change in her disposition, I would've considered her leaving dishes and not feeling the need to clean up, a win. Now, I was fraught with worry over her depressed state. If it continued once we received the results, some kind of intervention would be needed. For today, I'd continue giving her the space she so obviously wanted, acknowledging there probably hadn't been many times in her life she'd had the freedom to take it.

While Pearl remained unwilling to leave the cabin, I'd spent my time pouring over anything I could get my hands on concerning both the Aryan Nation and the ABT. I didn't find any new information; instead, I scoured old reports, hoping a new "clue" would jump out at me that might lead me to discover why Luke Howell believed the Nation would find Pearl valuable.

Hoping to be able to share some kind of news with her over breakfast, I called Hammer to see if he'd received the results. I anticipated he'd give me shit about calling, while reminding me that if he had the results, I'd hear from him. I called anyway, but he didn't pick up. When I still hadn't heard from him an hour after we finished lunch, I sent a text. That went unanswered as well.

When my phone did ring, it was with a call from Vex. I'd been waiting to hear from him since I arrived in Colorado, and that it took him so long to respond pissed me off. "About time," I snapped. "Why the fuck haven't you checked in?"

"There's something brewing here, within the ABT. I've felt increasingly shut out, but this morning, Shredder was finally able to get word to me. Scottie and I are under heavy suspicion, and reports of Pearl never arriving in Idaho are being circulated."

"What have you heard from your contacts at the Nation?"

"Nothing from up there yet, and our agents are well placed."

"Copy that. What's your plan?"

"Scottie suggested alerting the Nation about the major unrest down here and calling for reinforcements."

"Good idea. It will solidify your cover as being someone important on the national level."

"I haven't figured out how to neutralize the rumors about Pearl yet."

"We should have the DNA results today. Maybe something will come of that."

"Understood."

"Vex, before you end the call, if this situation escalates, get yourself and Scottie out of there."

"Roger that."

After hanging up, I was about to reach out to Hammer again when Fury's name popped up on my screen.

"Hey," I answered.

"Hey, Rip. Hammer asked me to give you a call. He's with Maeve at the hospital."

"Is everything okay?"

"She's having a baby, right?"

"Yeah, but it's early, isn't it?"

"Um…he didn't say. However, he did want me to let you know the results of Pearl's DNA test are in. I'm on my way to Colorado now."

"Why? Just tell me what they are."

"No confirmed hits on her parents yet, but I'm under orders to fly out now."

"Fury—"

"*Orders,* Rip. I'll explain when I get there." She ended the call.

"What the fuck?" I muttered, staring at the phone.

"What happened?" Pearl's eyes were wide.

"Fury is on her way here." I was still processing everything I'd learned in the last five minutes, and when I didn't elaborate, I expected Pearl to go back into the bedroom. Instead, she approached me.

"Why?"

"Why what?"

"Why is she on her way here?"

"She said she'd explain when she arrived." The other thing she'd said was there were no confirmed hits on who Pearl's parents were. The key word was *confirmed.* That meant there was a hit, but she wasn't authorized to tell me what it was.

I set my phone down and pulled her into a hug when I realized Pearl was shaking. "Shh, now. It's going to be okay. Whatever we find out, I'll be with you to process."

Pearl's tears dampened my shirt, and I realized my error in letting her withdraw over the last couple of days. While I believed I was doing the right thing by giving her space and time on her own, what I realized now, holding her as she sobbed, was the stress she was experiencing was on the edge of debilitating.

"I'm sorry, darlin'," I soothed, stroking her hair as she continued to cry.

"I'm…so…scared," she stammered.

"It's understandable you would be." I wouldn't tell her it wasn't. She was entitled to every damn thing she was feeling. Whether I believed it was logical or warranted didn't matter. More importantly, it was both of those things. Over the last several days, Pearl's entire life had been upended. She'd been ripped away from everything she knew, everything she believed about herself. Whether the way she'd been forced to live her life was right or wrong, it had still been her life. Her way of existence.

I led her over to the couch, sat down, and pulled her onto my lap. Pearl stopped crying and rested her head against my shoulder.

"I'm sorry I've been so rude to you the last three days."

"You took the time you needed. I'm glad you did. It means you felt free enough to do so."

I felt her nod. "It's like I lost my dad all over again."

"He'll always be the man who raised you."

"He was kind to me."

I expected Pearl to retreat to the bedroom, but she didn't. We spent the next few hours quietly, neither of us talking much, and when we did, it wasn't about anything important.

"Can we take a walk?" she asked after we'd finished eating lunch.

The weather was mild today, and the sun was out, making it feel warmer than the forty-five degrees it was. That was the thing about being in the mountain, particularly at almost nine-thousand-feet elevation; the sun was a lot more intense than at sea level.

"It's really beautiful here," she commented when we walked to a crest that gave us a view of the entire valley.

"I've always thought so."

"Prettier than Texas."

"In some ways."

I saw a vehicle headed in our direction and figured it was one of the hands doing afternoon chores. As it got closer, I saw Cord was driving and Fury was in the front passenger seat. While I'd been anxious to know the test results earlier, now I wished Pearl and I could have a few more hours before she was forced to face what could be unsettling news.

I reached over and took her hand in mine. "Fury is here."

"I know."

"We should walk back to the cabin."

She nodded. "I wish we didn't have to."

"I was just thinking the same thing."

Pearl looked up at me. "You were? Why?"

"I guess because if I had the ability to spare you heartache, I would."

I smiled when she squeezed my hand and murmured her thanks.

Cord and Fury were waiting on the porch when Pearl and I walked up to the cabin. Their conversation appeared animated, but Fury sobered the minute she saw us.

"I'll be on my way," said Cord, noticing us too. "It was nice to meet you, ma'am." He tipped his hat at Fury.

"I'll never get used to people calling me ma'am. Every time it happens, I want to tell whoever said it that I'm not old enough to be called that."

"Come on in," I said, opening the door for her and Pearl. "Can I get you ladies anything to eat or drink?" I poured a pitcher of water and set glasses on the table after both women declined anything.

"I'll get right to it," Fury began after I'd taken a seat between the two women. "There is a fifty percent DNA match in the system."

"Mother or father?" I asked.

"Father. His name is John Clinton."

My stomach sunk, but the results shouldn't have surprised me. The former leader of the Aryan Nation had been ousted from power by the current council of three almost thirty years ago.

"Should that mean something to me?" Pearl asked.

While I explained who he was, I couldn't tell her why her father's identity would make her of value to the current Nation leadership. Clinton was in prison and would be for life. Here in Colorado, in fact, three hours from Crested Butte.

Fury looked between me and Pearl, who was ghostly pale. "Do you have any questions?"

"How long will you be here on the ranch?" I asked, knowing full well that wasn't the kind of question she was looking for, especially when she glared in my direction.

"At least a few days."

"Where are you staying?"

"Cord put my things in the cabin next door."

I hadn't realized until she said it that she didn't appear to have anything with her.

"Unless Pearl has questions, we'll let you get settled."

Pearl didn't respond, not even to look at either of us.

"Don't get up," said Fury, pushing back her chair.

Since doing so meant I'd have to let go of Pearl's hand, I didn't.

"Let's sit on the couch," I suggested once we were alone. Like earlier, when I sat, I pulled her onto my lap. "Is there anything you want to talk about? Do you have any questions?"

"I don't think so."

I had plenty of my own, but none more than what the hell Luke Howell knew that I wasn't piecing together.

I'd lost track of how much time had passed while Pearl and I looked at the logs stacked in the unlit fireplace. I remained quiet, not wanting to interrupt her thoughts.

"I wish it was my mother instead," she whispered.

"I hoped for the same thing."

"I wish I could ask him about her."

Could she? Not just that question, but also if he had any idea why the Nation would want to know who or where she was, and how she'd ended up with Fischer.

If the man who had raised her was a known associate of Clinton's, wouldn't he have been on the national organization's radar? Wouldn't the ABT have been the first place they looked for him or Pearl?

"Would you like to try to see him?"

Pearl raised her head to look at me. "Is that possible?"

Clinton was in what was considered the highest security level of any prison, intended for particularly dangerous inmates. I had no idea what visitation policies would be in place. If any visits were allowed, I would think one from a child, even an adult daughter, would be the type permitted.

"I can find out. Would you like me to do that now?"

When she said she would, I shifted her off my lap and walked over to the kitchen to get my computer. I picked up my phone and saw there was a new message from Fury.

New report: 25 percent match to John Fischer.

A percentage match in that range typically meant the person was either an aunt, uncle, or cousin. It was a connection that made sense but, again, didn't explain why Fischer hadn't been on the council of three's radar.

Shredder have any luck with Howell? I messaged Vex.

I wasn't surprised not to receive a quick response. It could be hours before I got one. I stuck my phone in my pocket and set my laptop on the coffee table in front of where Pearl waited.

"Would you like me to light the fireplace?" I asked when I noticed her rubbing her arms.

"Yes, please."

I waited until it was lit, then took a seat beside her to relay the latest development. "I received another message from Fury. The test results indicate that John Fischer may have been your uncle."

For the first time since we'd gone to Gunnison to have the DNA test performed, Pearl's expression looked hopeful. I suppose it would be good news to her to find out she was actually related to the man. That information also made getting an audience with Clinton more compelling. Was Fischer his brother living under an alias we hadn't uncovered, or was he Pearl's mother's sibling?

18

Pearl

I couldn't explain why I felt relief, knowing the man I thought was my father was my uncle, but I did. At least it made sense that he'd treated me so well. I was a relation, even though I wasn't his daughter.

The other thing I couldn't explain was why I had an overwhelming feeling that I was about to find out something about my mother. I'd been disappointed when Fury said the match was for my father, even though it's what I expected.

"It is possible for your father to have visitors," Rip said, pointing at something he was reading on his computer. I leaned forward to read it myself.

"Visits to the penitentiary occur on Thursdays, Fridays, weekends, and federal holidays. Visiting hours are from 8:00 A.M. to 3:00 P.M. on each of these days. A prisoner is allowed five visits per month. One visit can last up to seven hours; however, visits may be terminated if overcrowding occurs in the visiting room. Inmates can have no more than three visitors at once, including children."

"I'll have Fury make the arrangements if you think you want to do this," Rip offered.

"I do want to." Today was Saturday, which meant it could happen as soon as tomorrow. I thought I'd feel nervous about it, like I had when we waited for the test results, but I didn't. "Thank you," I said, resting my head on Rip's shoulder. He leaned over and kissed my hair like I'd seen Hammer do with Maeve. I wrapped my arm around him and squeezed.

"You seem happy," he commented.

"I can't explain it," I said, giving voice to how I'd been feeling.

"I was worried about you."

"I'm sorry—"

"Don't be," he interrupted. "While I wished there was something I could do to make you feel better or less anxious or whatever it was you were experiencing, another part of me was happy you felt comfortable enough putting your dishes in the sink and walking away."

I raised my head and leaned back so I could see his face. "Me putting my dishes in the sink made you happy?"

He laughed and nodded. "It meant you trusted me not to get upset with you for it."

I had to admit, him getting upset hadn't even occurred to me. I also had to admit it wasn't something I ever would've gotten away with at the compound. "I guess that means I feel free when I'm with you."

Rip leaned forward and kissed me. "That is the greatest compliment you could give me, darlin'."

There was a knock at the door, and Rip shifted to get up. "That will be Fury. I sent her a message, asking about a prison visit."

While he opened the door, I went into the kitchen. I hadn't been too hungry the last couple of days, but now, I felt famished. We'd eaten all the BBQ food Flynn had left for us, but there were still plenty of other things to choose from.

"Hi," I said when the woman walked over to the kitchen table. Out of everyone I'd met through Rip, she was the only person who intimidated me, and that included the men. Was it because I knew she'd had some kind of relationship with Rip, or was it just her demeanor? I definitely wouldn't call her warm or friendly.

"Hey," she responded, walking over to where I was putting fruit on a plate. "Can I help?"

"Um…sure," I said rather than tell her I was almost finished.

"There's so much food over at my place. Let me know if you want any of it."

"Flynn didn't leave any barbecue or potato salad, did she?"

Fury's eyes opened wide. "Enough to feed ten people. I don't even eat meat. Do you want me to go get it?"

"I can go," offered Rip. "Did you leave the door unlocked?"

The look Fury gave him when she handed him the key made me laugh out loud. "Would you have left it unlocked?" she asked me once he walked out.

I shrugged. "I haven't paid any attention, to be honest. Where I lived before, doors were rarely locked."

"Fair enough." She leaned up against the counter. "How are you doing? I mean, this is a lot to take in."

"Okay, I guess. People have been so kind to me."

"Rip especially." She smiled and wriggled her eyebrows.

"Look, I'm sorry if you and he—"

She held up a hand. "He and I weren't anything, Pearl. I promise. I haven't exactly been sitting around, waiting for Rip to call me for the last few months. Even less so before that."

"Do you have another man?"

"Hmm. Have him? Not sure about that. There is a man I'm interested in. It's casual, though."

"Yeah?"

We both stopped talking when we heard Rip's footsteps on the porch.

"I'll tell you more about him later," she whispered. "I'll say this much, though. He's hot as fuck."

I knew my cheeks flamed pink and hated that they had. Fury didn't comment, though.

"You handle the meat, and I'll do the salads," she said when Rip set the containers of food on the counter. "Don't you have something else to do?" she added when he maneuvered around us to help.

"Like what?"

"I don't know, but this kitchen is too small for three people."

"You could go find something else to do," he snapped back at her.

"Or you could share Pearl's company for five minutes. You have been hogging her all to yourself."

He leaned over and kissed my cheek. "And I'll keep doing it as long as she lets me."

I was so unused to this kind of attention that it made me a little uncomfortable. More, though, it made me feel happy. Not that many people on the compound *wanted* to spend time with me.

Rip didn't leave, but he did sit down at the table. "What have you found out about visiting Clinton?" he asked.

"Oh! That's what I came over to tell you. We can go tomorrow if you'd like. He's never had visitors, not even once—other than his attorney, which doesn't count—so he hasn't reached his limit."

"Will he see me?" I asked.

"I don't know, but I did send a message, asking."

"We should probably get an answer before we make the drive."

My eyes met Rip's. "How far is it?" I asked him.

"Three hours."

I nodded, knowing he was right but trying really hard not to let myself get sad about it. If this man refused to see me, I'd be crushed, but there was no point in being upset until that happened. If it happened.

Fury's phone made a noise, and she walked over to the table where it sat. She picked it up and looked at the screen. "He consented to a visit," she said, her eyes meeting mine. "Tomorrow, then?"

"Yes, please."

Rip stood and walked over to the couch. He motioned with his head for me to join him. Fury picked up on it.

"I've got another call to make, so I'll go next door."

"You don't have to leave," I said, figuring she only wanted to give us privacy.

"Remember that person I told you about earlier?"

I nodded.

"That's who I'm calling. You sure you want me to do it from here?"

I laughed. "Probably not."

"Yeah, I didn't think so."

"I don't even want to know," Rip said after she left.

"What did you want to talk to me about?"

"I'd like to be with you when you meet with Clinton."

It hadn't occurred to me that he might not be. "I'd like that too."

"What would you think of Fury being with us?"

"I wouldn't mind, but why?"

Rip took a deep breath and let it out slowly. "She used to be with the CIA, like I was. My main focus is going to be on how you're doing. I'd like her to focus on whatever information Clinton gives us."

"Why do you care so much about me?"

"You're easy to care about."

I cocked my head. "That really isn't an answer."

He smiled. "It is if it's true. You care about me, don't you?"

"Yes."

"Why?"

While I didn't answer, Rip knew he'd made his point. Caring about someone didn't need a reason. It was a feeling. Was it naive of me to hope he'd never stop?

19

Rip

The thing about Pearl was she was so much stronger than she realized. As we stood in the visitation room the next morning, waiting for her father to join us, her shoulders were back, her chin up, her head held high. No matter what happened with the man she was about to meet, the message she was sending was that she wasn't afraid. She'd come for answers about her life, and she intended to get them. While I had no right to be, I was proud of her.

Out of the corner of my eye, I caught Fury studying me but didn't turn to look at her. The only connection I wanted in the room was with Pearl. Fury knew what was expected of her. She was here to watch Clinton, pay attention to every nuance, decide whether any information he gave us was true or a lie.

Before we left the Roaring Fork just after dawn, Pearl and I talked about what she wanted to happen during this meeting. If she was only able to get the answer to one question, what would it be?

She didn't respond right away, but when she did, it was about her mother. "I want to know who she is."

It was a good answer. I'd said "one question." Asking whether she was alive or dead wouldn't tell Pearl what she needed to know. Who she was, would. If we knew her identity, we might be able to find out on our own whether she was still living.

I didn't want to give Pearl unfounded hope, but now that we knew who her father was, Fury confirmed someone on the Invincibles team was looking for whatever records they could find—places where the man had lived, marriage records, and whether he was listed on any birth certificates.

Pearl's quick intake of breath was audible when the door opened and a man in shackles was led into the room about the size of the one we were in but on the other side of a wall with only a small double-paned window between them. His eyes went straight to his daughter's, and she kept her gaze steady.

The two guards who'd escorted him led him to a table made of concrete similar to the one in the room we were in. After he was seated, one attached the shackles of his hands to something on the table. The other guard bent down to tie his legs, I assumed, although I couldn't see to know for certain.

When the first guard flipped a switch, we could hear noise from the other side of the wall.

"Hello," said Pearl, taking a seat at the table.

The man continued to study her but didn't speak.

"I'm your daughter."

He gave a slight nod that would've been easy to miss if I hadn't been studying him.

"My name is Pearl, and I want to know who my mother is."

When after two or three minutes, the man still hadn't uttered a single word, Pearl got flustered for the first time since this morning.

"Are you going to say anything?" she demanded. "Do you know my life is in danger? Do you know the ABT also had my DNA tested, so they probably know you're my father too? They want to trade me to the Aryan Brotherhood. For what, I don't know. Do you know why?"

The man shook his head, again just slightly.

Pearl looked up at the guards standing near the back of the room where her father sat mute. "Can he speak?" she asked.

The guard nodded but didn't say a word, either.

"They were going to kill me. Do you know that?" She shook her head when he still didn't respond. He did, however, keep his eyes glued to her. "They already killed the man I thought was my father."

That wasn't exactly true, and Pearl knew it. Maybe her goal, though, was to provoke some kind of reaction from him. She looked over her shoulder at me. "Can you please leave us alone?"

She would certainly be safe on her own, and while earlier, my biggest concern was how she'd handle this meeting, after watching her with him, I was no longer worried. When the visit came to an end, I'd be waiting to soothe her if she needed me to.

"Yes," I answered simply, ignoring the look Fury was shooting at me. "Let's go," I said to her, motioning to the door.

"Do you think this is a good idea?" she whispered as she brushed by me.

"I'll be right outside," I told Pearl rather than answer Fury.

"I'll be okay."

I pressed the button on the intercom like the guard had showed us when we came in. Seconds later, the door clicked, and I was able to open it. Once it shut behind us, I kept watch on Pearl through its small window.

"I asked you a question," Fury reminded me.

"I obviously thought she'd be okay, or I wouldn't have agreed to it. There is a chance her instincts are right, and maybe he'll tell her something if we aren't in the room."

Less than five minutes later, I saw Pearl stand. It didn't appear her father had said any more after we left than he did when we were with her. She was halfway between the desk where she'd been seated and the door where I stood and watched from, when she came to an abrupt stop. She spun back around. I could see Clinton was saying something but had no idea what it might be.

Pearl nodded, turned back in my direction, and pressed the button on the intercom. I stepped aside when I heard the lock click.

Once she was through the door, I held my arms open and she walked into them. "I'm sorry, Pearl. I know you'd hoped for more from him."

"I don't know why I did. It wasn't like my dad—err, uncle—ever told me about him or gave me a message from him, or anything. After twenty-eight years of silence, why should I have expected him to talk?"

"What did he say when you were leaving?"

"Six words. 'Do you still have your bear?' That's it. Do I still have my bear? Obviously, he must've been the one to give it to me. What was I supposed to do? Thank him?"

My eyes met Fury's over Pearl's head. If my gut was right, John Clinton had just given Pearl the answers she was looking for—at least some of them.

The return drive through the prison complex and to the ranch was quiet. Pearl didn't speak, and neither did Fury nor I. Even when we pulled up to the cabins and parted ways, no one said a word.

Once inside, I lit a fire before taking a seat next to Pearl on the couch.

"How are you doing?" I asked, gathering her into my arms, relieved when she rested her head on my chest.

"I thought about that question a lot on our way here. I'm not sure I have an answer."

"Understandable."

"He looked dead. Like he had no life inside him."

"His future is bleak at best."

Even I hadn't known what to expect from the maximum-security prison, and what I saw wasn't at all the way I imagined it. First, it seemed as though we were in the wrong place.

We'd checked in at a gate close to the road, then drove for over ten miles, past several other federal prisons, before being met by two black SUVs blocking us from going any farther.

We left my vehicle in one of only three parking places and were transported by one of the SUVs that had blocked us. I looked behind us to see the second followed us through the next series of gates, each with a manned guardhouse.

We were dropped off at another building, too small to be more than a check-in center, although I couldn't see any other structures on the horizon in front of us.

After signing in again, we were led down a long flight of stairs made of solid concrete and over to an elevator that took us down farther. The entire process, from the first check-in until we were escorted into the room where Pearl first laid eyes on her father, took over an hour.

"I didn't feel any connection to him, if that's what you're asking."

"He was very closed off."

"Out of everything he could've said to me, why did he ask me about a stupid teddy bear?"

"I have a theory about that."

Pearl sat up. "You do? What?"

"The bear is important somehow."

"Okay."

"Where is it? In the bedroom?"

"Do you want me to get it?" she asked.

"If you wouldn't mind."

She returned holding the stuffed animal much like she had the first time I saw her with it.

"May I see it?"

When Pearl handed me the bear, I gently squeezed the stuffing until I felt a small, hard object.

"What is it?" she asked, studying my actions.

"Something hard."

"I figured it was the thing that made it talk."

"Did it talk?"

"Not that I remember. I just assumed it was busted."

I set the bear on the coffee table and looked into Pearl's eyes. "I need to open it up and see what it is."

"Okay."

"You're sure?"

Her eyes scrunched. "Are you making fun of me?"

"Not at all. I just want to be sure you're okay if I rip open something so important to you."

She made a funny face. "I can always sew it back up, can't I?"

"Well, yeah."

This time Pearl rolled her eyes. "Do you want me to do it?"

I laughed. "Actually, yes."

She stood and walked into the kitchen, returning with a pair of scissors, which she used to carefully open a seam. The opening didn't have to be very big for her to reach in and pull out the exact thing I guessed it would be—a DDS data cartridge. While when Pearl was a child, the technology was at least four or five years old, it had still been widely used for data storage.

The issue now was, first, finding a reader for it, and second, it hadn't been a reliable storage methodology back in the day, let alone now.

Regardless, we had to try to access whatever was on it. As soon as Pearl said Clinton had asked about the bear, I knew the reason was because of the importance of what we'd find inside it.

I called the only person I could think of who would know the fastest way for me to access that cartridge's data.

"Hey, Rip. How goes it on the Roaring Fork?" asked Decker Ashford, answering my call before it even rang on my end. The guy wasn't just the head of the Invincibles—at least in the US—and my ultimate boss; he was also a technological genius. He was the kind of guy you'd think would've been a complete nerd in high school instead of the badass I'd heard he was.

"I've stumbled on something that may contain information needed for the ABT mission."

"That is excellent news. What did you find?"

"A DDS."

"Shit. Been a while since I've seen one of those suckers."

"I don't know where to look to get access to what's on it."

"This may take me a minute. Hang tight." My cell rang minutes later. "Look, depending on what's on this thing, I don't want it getting in someone's hands who could compromise the DAT itself. I'm also not going to risk having it get lost in transit. Crash is on his way to Gunnison now."

"Roger that, sir. I'll deliver the cartridge directly to him."

"You'll deliver the cartridge directly to me, Rip. I understand the reasoning behind you relocating to Colorado, or I wouldn't have authorized the use of the jet. However, I can keep you and Miss Pearl safe between Austin-Bergstrom and King-Alexander. Once you're there, no one will touch a hair on that woman's head."

"I don't doubt that, sir—"

"Yeah, yeah. Get your ass to Gunnison in under two hours, and we'll talk more when you get here."

"What's happening?" Pearl asked with wide eyes.

"We're returning to Texas."

"When?"

"As soon as the plane gets here."

Pearl held up her bear. "I checked, and there isn't anything else inside the patient other than stuffing. Can I stitch him up?"

I smiled. "Get at it, doc."

20

Pearl

Sure, meeting my biological father had rattled me, but not as much as I thought it would. The primary emotion I felt was anger, especially when he refused to talk. Now, I was just appreciative he'd asked about my stuffed bear.

Rip had warned me the thing we found inside Mojo might not be usable. "These types of data storage are notoriously faulty," he'd said. However, he also said his boss was optimistic enough that it would contain important information that he wanted us to return to Texas and bring it with us. I didn't know much of anything about airplanes, but it had to cost a lot of money to use them.

As far as what "important" information was on the thing, all I cared about was whether there was anything about my mother. I couldn't explain the feeling I had, but I just *knew* we were going to find out who she was.

One other thing dawned on me. If John Fischer was my uncle, he must not have been John Clinton's brother. Who would name both their kids the same thing, and why would they have different last names? While this was another subject I knew little about, I hoped it meant he was my mother's brother.

I wasn't any less scared on the plane ride from Colorado to Texas. In fact, it was a lot bumpier than the first one had been. Rip reassured me it was normal, but I was greatly relieved when we landed.

There was an SUV waiting for us near the plane like there had been in Colorado. Rip introduced the man driving it as his boss, Decker Ashford. I thought Hammer was his boss, but maybe that was just at the ranch.

Mr. Ashford was very nice and funny, too. He had both Rip and me laughing the whole way from the airport into the city, where we dropped Fury off at her house, to another ranch called King-Alexander.

"This will be your base for the time being while I figure out what's on the DDS," he said. "Pearl, there are security protocols in place here that are more complex than what may have been on the ABT compound or on the Hammered Dubliner. Make sure if you decide to go for a walk, Rip is with you."

"Yes, sir," I responded. My cheeks flamed, wondering if he knew I walked alone from Rip's place to Hammer's the morning we left for Colorado. I hoped not. I wouldn't want Rip to get in any kind of trouble for it. I'd wait until we were alone to ask, though.

When Mr. Ashford said we'd be staying in the east guesthouse, Rip raised his eyebrows and thanked him. Even then, I hadn't expected it to be as grand as it looked when we drove up to it and he said, "Here we are."

"This is a guesthouse?" I asked, feeling silly as soon as I had. It obviously was, since he'd said it was where we were staying.

"I've never stayed in this one," Rip admitted, seeming as impressed by it as I was.

"About the only one empty presently, but even if it wasn't, I figured it would be a nice getaway since I'd advise against you returning to the Hammered Dubliner, at least for now."

He helped us take our bags inside and told Rip he'd be in touch about what he found on the thing that was inside Mojo.

"I don't know about you, but I'm pretty hungry."

"I can make us something," I said, eyeing the fancy kitchen.

"Or we can make something together." Rip winked.

While I was more used to it than when I first left the compound, it was still hard to remember that I wasn't expected to make all the food or clean or do any other chores all on my own.

When Rip opened the refrigerator, I was surprised to see how much food was in it. "I make a pretty mean omelet. Sound good?" he asked.

"I've never made an omelet. At the compound, it was just easier to add things to scrambled eggs."

"That's what my omelets end up looking like."

"What are they supposed to look like?"

He got out his phone and pulled up a photo. When he tapped it, another screen opened with a recipe.

"You can get recipes on your phone?"

"Sure can."

"And it turns on lights." I shook my head in amazement.

"I'll see about getting you one tomorrow morning. I should've thought of it sooner."

"Me?" What did I need a phone for? It wasn't like I had anyone to call. "I don't think I'd use it."

"You'll be surprised how much you will. For example, Hammer could've sent this directly to you." He tapped something else on the screen, and a photo of a baby popped up. At the bottom, it read, "Mary Maeve Anderson. Weight: 5 lbs., 15 ounces. 19 inches long."

"She's so beautiful," I gasped, and my eyes filled with tears.

Rip laughed. "If you say so. Kind of looks like an alien to me."

I swatted him. "Don't ever let a mother hear you say that, especially Maeve."

Rip made us omelets while I sat at the counter, looking at the photo of Maeve's baby. I nearly jumped out of my seat when a message popped up on the screen that read, *I'm in!!!*

I got up and handed Rip the phone. "I think you should look at this."

He raised a brow. "That was quick."

"Was it from Mr. Ashford?"

"It was."

The phone went off again, and this time, based on the look on Rip's face, it wasn't good news.

Rip

Things are escalating quickly. Trying to get Scottie to leave the compound now, read the text Vex sent via HALE. There were things about what he'd said I didn't like. First, that he'd used the word "trying." Second, that he'd said he was trying to only get Scottie to leave the compound. If things were escalating to that point, he should be leaving as well.

Abort mission and evacuate now, was the return message I sent. *Direct order. You, Scottie, and Shredder. Confirm whether backup is needed.*

I waited, but there was no immediate response. I turned the heat off on the stove and plated our dinner, keeping a constant watch on my phone at the same time. The next message I received was from Decker, saying he was on his way here.

Trouble at the compound, I responded, including Money in the thread. *Issued evacuation orders. Requesting authorization to mobilize on the ABT front.*

I received an almost immediate response from Money, granting the authorization I'd requested. Simultaneously, a message from Decker came with the recommendation the team in place at the Aryan Nation also mobilize based on recent intel he'd received. That thread included the point people for this mission at both the FBI and DHS along with Money and me. I assumed the intel Decker referred to was whatever was on the DDS, but I wasn't certain that was all it was.

A few minutes later, I saw Decker's SUV pull into the drive and waited by the door to let him in. When I turned around, I noticed Pearl had left the room.

"I'll get to what's on the DDS in a minute, but first, we need to deal with what's happening at the compound. I've lost connection to both eyes and ears, and I don't *lose* connections. Either Vex terminated both intentionally, or someone else did." Decker sat on a stool at the kitchen counter and opened his laptop. "Still dark."

"I have a team on standby that I'm ready to mobilize."

"Who've you got?" he asked.

"Jagger, Steel, Rock, Ink, and Rage."

"Crash and Angel are available too. They're here on the ranch. Fury should be read in on this one too."

"Roger that," I said, sending her the same message I'd sent to everyone else.

She responded right away, copying both Hammer, Decker, and me, requesting permission to assist.

"What are your thoughts?" I asked him.

"We'll keep her on standby."

"Roger that," I said after sending her a response with that directive.

"Before you move out, I found something you need to be aware of, going in. I have reason to believe Pearl's mother is living on the ABT compound. Has been the whole time."

I spun around when I heard her gasp.

"I'm sorry. I came out to use the bathroom," she stammered before covering her mouth with her hand.

"Don't be," Decker told her. "I want you to hear this too."

When he went into the living room, Pearl and I followed. We sat in stunned silence as Decker laid out the information he'd gotten off the DDS.

John Clinton had managed to conceal the identity of both his daughter and her mother as soon as he realized the woman was pregnant. There was already enough unrest in the Nation that he feared for their safety.

He called upon John Fischer, who Clinton had met in prison and whom he'd met Pearl's mother through. Fischer moved the two around for several months before finally settling them both at the ABT compound—he and the baby first, followed by his sister a few weeks later.

"Who is she?" Pearl asked.

"That information was not included, nor was your complete birth certificate."

"What do you mean by complete?" I asked.

"It shows Pearl's name and date of birth, but the mother's and father's names as well as the year have been redacted."

"What is redacted?" she asked.

"Obscured or marked out in such a way it's unreadable," Decker responded.

"What about the name of the hospital?" I asked.

"Also redacted."

"You said it showed my date of birth?"

"That's right."

"What is it?"

"April 3."

Pearl's eyes filled with tears.

"What's wrong?" I whispered.

"I never knew."

I hated the ABT motherfuckers already and didn't have a very high opinion of Pearl's father or her uncle. My opinion of her mother remained to be seen since the woman had allegedly lived in close proximity to her daughter and never acknowledged her. Hearing that Pearl hadn't even known her own birthday, increased the intense dislike I had of her family.

"If things have escalated at the compound to the point where Vex and Scottie can't get off the property, then we should assume the splinter group has mobilized. If they know Pearl is John Clinton's daughter, there's a chance they know who her mother is as well."

Decker nodded and murmured his agreement while, at the same time, studying something on his computer. "I've got eyes, although spotty. No ears yet. It doesn't look good, Rip."

I stood and looked at the images he was staring at, and it looked like a war zone.

"We need to mobilize now," said Decker. "I brought tactical gear for you and for me, anticipating this. Crash should arrive any minute and will head out with us. Angel will be with him, but rather than go to the compound, I want her to stay here with Pearl." Deck tossed me his keys. "Grab our gear."

As I was walking out of the house, I heard him ask Pearl if there was anything at all she could remember that may give us a clue to her mother's identity. I couldn't hear her response, but the next thing I heard him say was, "If you think of anything, even the most minute detail that would help us identify who she is, have Angel relay the information to the team immediately."

I brought in the gear and suited up, unsure I'd have even a few minutes alone with Pearl before Decker and I had to leave.

"You and I will be on standby right outside the compound for transport or backup," said Decker when he came out after donning his own gear.

"But—"

"Direct order, Rip."

"Roger that, sir," I muttered.

"Crash's ETA is under a minute. As soon as he arrives, we'll head out. I'll be waiting in the SUV."

"I know you're scared," I said to Pearl as soon as the door closed behind Deck. "Angel will be here with you."

Pearl's eyes were wide, and she blinked back tears. "I wish she was going with you instead."

"Why?"

"Then you'd have an angel watching over you."

I kissed her. "I'll be back as soon as I can."

"I've never been much of a praying woman, but I'll be saying some for you, Rip."

Jagger and Steel were the first to arrive at the rendezvous point, followed by Decker, Crash, and myself, then Rage and Ink. "Rock is on his way," reported Ink. "He said he'd join us in position as soon as he could; just relay the coordinates of where you want him to be."

I pulled out the map of the compound and went over each person's orders. "Your targets are specific and limited. This is an extraction op, not a raid. We want to get Vex, Scottie, and Shredder out. Crash, I want you on Shredder. Jagger and Steel, your assignment is to find Vex. Knock the fucker out and drag him from that compound if you have to."

Both smiled and nodded.

"Rage and Ink. Your assignment is to get Scottie out."

Once Rock arrived, I'd get with Decker again about going in myself. It would take two of us, at least, to find a person whose identity was a mystery.

"Our fourth and final target is unknown." I explained that Pearl's mother was believed to be living on the compound under an alias, but who she really was may have been discovered. If that was the case, she was in danger of being used in the same way Howell and the others in his splinter group had planned to use Pearl.

What they were after, I was certain, was what we'd found inside Pearl's teddy bear. From what little Decker said on the ride over, there was enough evidence on the DDS to take down the council of three at the national level as well as many of its members and those of the Texas chapter.

The team was just about to move out when Rock arrived. He had Edge with him.

"Since Edge is also here, I'd like to respectfully request I go in with Rock, sir," I said to Decker.

Edge responded rather than the man I made the request of. "Request denied. Long before this became your op, it was mine. I want this settled and the ABT ended. I can't sit on my hands while others do my job."

Decker looked at me and nodded. I didn't like it, but I'd been overruled on two fronts. I knew better than to argue further.

We equipped those going into the compound with the same devices Deck had supplied on the other part of this op, when our primary mission was to extract Maeve. The devices allowed for audio and video recording through a smart contact lens that went in one eye only. Starting and ending the recording was controlled by a blink pattern, as were zoom and volume.

Sight and sound were then transmitted to Decker's computer, where through individual windows, we could watch the action in the same way we would be able to if there were surveillance cameras mounted throughout the compound.

Once the team moved in, what we saw still looked like a war zone. Visuals were limited. The compound was mostly obscured by smoke but probably from smoke bombs rather than fire.

"Any sign of Vex, Scottie, or Shredder?" Decker asked through the comm.

"Negative on Vex," Jagger responded.

"Negative on Scottie," said Ink.

"Nothing on Shredder either," said Crash.

The next voice we heard, but through the computer's audio, was Angel's, saying Pearl believed if anyone on the compound was her mother, the most likely person was a woman named Opal.

"Description?" Edge responded.

"What do you think? Maybe five feet four?" said a voice from behind us. By the time Decker and I spun around in its direction, I counted six of what looked like FN Herstals trained on us.

22

Pearl

"She's even more beautiful in person," I exclaimed when Angel opened the door, invited Hammer and Maeve inside, and I rushed over to see the baby.

"Aye," said Maeve, cooing at her daughter. "She's perfect."

Hammer kissed his wife's temple, then his baby's forehead. "I've got some business to attend to. I'll be back as soon as I can."

"Be safe, husband. Mary Maeve and I are counting on you."

"You know it," he said before walking back out the way he'd come in.

"Where's he going?" I asked.

"To the ABT compound."

"I was afraid that's what you were going to say. Have you heard anything?"

Maeve shook her head and looked over at Angel. "Hello, I don't believe we've met."

The other woman took a step forward. "We have. I'm Teagon Evans, pilot for the Invincibles."

"Oh, right. A Brit. Forgive me, pregnancy brain."

Angel laughed. "It's all right. Can I bring you anything?"

"I'd love a cup of tea. You don't have chamomile, do you?"

Angel looked at me, and I shrugged. "I've only been here a little over an hour."

"I'll look. You two sit and relax."

I was so tired I didn't argue.

"Would you like to hold her?" Maeve asked when I sat beside her and Angel said she'd found some tea.

"I'd love to, if you wouldn't mind."

"Goodness, no. You look like you could use a *cwtch*."

"A what?"

"A cuddle," Angel answered.

"That was quick. I didn't hear the kettle boil," said Maeve when Angel delivered the tea.

"There's a hot-water dispenser by the sink," she explained. "Fancy a cup?" she asked me.

Maeve took a sip. "There's no caffeine, so it won't keep you or my little one up."

"I can get it."

"You've got the baby. Stay where you are, and I'll get it," said Angel.

I would have loved every minute I was spending with Maeve, the baby, and Angel, who was just as nice as everyone else I'd met since I left the compound. I especially loved her accent, which was similar to Maeve's, but also noticeably different. However, all I could think about was Rip being at the compound.

"Have you heard anything?" I asked again, this time of Angel.

"Not yet, but as soon as I do, I'll let you know," she said, setting the cup of tea on the table in front of me.

"I didn't know how you like it."

"With a little cream, please." My eyes opened wide.

"What happened?" Maeve asked. "Something with the baby?"

"No. The tea. I never used to like it, but then someone at the compound suggested I try it with cream."

Maeve held out her arms when the baby started to cry. "Sorry, she's hungry."

I looked up at Angel. *"Ms. Opal."*

"She could be your mum?"

"Out of everyone on the compound, she's the only one who makes sense." Now that I thought about it, she had the same hair and eye color as John Fischer. Similar features too, from what I could remember.

The baby latched onto Maeve's breast. "What's this, then? Something about Ms. Opal? The one of the pancakes?"

"Decker—Mr. Ashford—asked if there was anything I could think of that might give them a clue as to who my mother might be."

"This is big news, Pearl," said Maeve, reaching over to hold my hand.

I heard Angel telling someone everything I'd just said. I caught a glimpse of her face right after she said the words.

"What?" I asked.

"Everything is fine."

I couldn't say why, but I knew she was lying, especially when her eyes remained riveted on her laptop. As much as I wanted to get up and look, I couldn't bring myself to. When Angel stood and carried her computer into the other room, I felt sick to my stomach.

"Everything will be okay," Maeve leaned over and whispered. "We have to believe that."

"I'm so scared," I whispered too.

"Pray, Pearl. Pray with all your heart." When Maeve closed her eyes and held my hand tighter, I did.

23

Rip

The other thing I saw, besides the weapons pointed directly at us, were Scottie and a woman I assumed was Pearl's mother, being held with guns to their heads. There was no sign of Vex; however, I made eye contact with Shredder, the one with the gun pressed against Scottie's temple.

"Raise your hands high in the air, boys," said one of the men with an automatic weapon pointed directly at me. "Grab the computer," I heard the guy holding Opal shout. At the same time, two gunshots rang out—one that sounded as though it was directly behind us, and the other behind the men poised to kill us.

Decker tossed the computer under the SUV when he and I dropped to the ground and began firing our own weapons. One by one, the ABTers fell, including the one holding Opal. He'd been taken out by Shredder. Scottie covered her while the gun battle raged on. Shots were coming from over Deck's head and mine while more were being fired from behind and to each side of our assailants.

By the time Edge called the all clear, it appeared all those on the team who'd gone into the compound had either surrounded us or run into the woods to check for additional gunmen. By my count, one man remained unaccounted for—Vex.

"What's the scene inside?" I asked.

"Hard to tell whether we're dealing with mass suicide or a total bloodbath," reported Ink. "When we realized the smoke was a cover for dead bodies, we heard the shots fired from out here."

"Who fired them?"

"Me," I heard a familiar voice say from behind me. What I wanted to do was punch Vex for taking out his own communication. Instead, I hugged the bastard.

"And me," I heard another voice say, walking toward us from the other direction and removing her helmet as she did.

Fury approached, and while I thought she was headed to me, Vex stepped forward, and the two high-fived.

I shook my head and walked over to the woman Scottie was helping up from the ground. "You're Opal, right?" I asked.

"Yes, sir," she responded through tears.

"Someone very special to me—and I think to you too—is looking forward to chatting with you. I'll take you to her just as soon as I can."

Before I could do that, though, I had a long list of questions I wanted answers to. So many, I didn't know where to begin.

Like, who the fuck authorized Fury when I'd told her to stand down until she received word from me? And what the fuck was up with Vex's continued lack of communication? However, I knew that if I started in, Decker would intervene and tell me these were things we would address in the hotwash.

"The cleaners are on their way." Deck motioned to the bodies scattered on the ground. "We've got a team made up of local law enforcement, BATFE, and the DOJ."

"Homeland too, sir," said Scottie. She was standing next to Vex, who had his arm around her shoulders.

"You and I have a few things to get straight," I said after motioning him away from her.

"I know how it looks, but it wasn't the way you or Deck think."

"Right. Are you saying Decker's equipment failed?"

"I'm saying the two men who nearly destroyed it are both lying in pools of blood, thanks to Scottie." Vex removed his NVDs, and I saw one of his eyes was nearly swollen closed.

"Let's get someone to take a look at that," Decker said, walking over to us.

Vex blinked a couple of times, brought his finger up to his eye, and popped the contact lens out. "See? Ready for its next assignment."

Decker squeezed his shoulder and chuckled. "Next time, worry more about your eye, son."

"Roger that," muttered Vex.

"What about Fury? Who authorized her involvement?"

Vex shrugged. "Wasn't me. I was too busy trying to keep Scottie and me alive."

"I did." The last person I expected to see walk up and join us was Hammer. "Sorry I'm late to the party, kids." He pulled his pocket humidor out and held it open in my direction. "I'd say you could use one of these and a few fingers of bourbon. You'll have to wait until you're back at King-Alexander for the juice, but you're welcome to light one up now."

I held up a hand. "Thanks, but I'll take a pass on the stogie."

"Can't say I didn't offer."

"I could go for one of those," said Vex.

Hammer raised a brow and stuck the humidor back in his pocket. "You'll get one as soon as it's your mission successfully completed. This one was Rip's, and don't you forget it."

I nudged him with my shoulder. "It was his just as much; I'll concede that."

Hammer turned to Decker. "What's this sharin' the credit crap? Somethin' new the Invincibles are doin'?"

Decker laughed. "Not the Invincibles, but maybe the new team will institute that policy."

"New team?" I asked.

"Yes, sir. The one you and Vex are heading up."

"You got Fury listed as attorney of record?" asked Hammer.

"Damn straight."

"Well, hell, stogies for all three of you, then."

"You know something I don't?" Vex leaned in and asked me.

"First I've heard of a new team, let alone heading it up."

"Not me," said Fury, joining us.

"Is that right?"

"Who do you think they asked to draw up the contracts?"

Hammer took out his pocket humidor, opened it, and held it out to me. "Before you turn it down again, take a look at the pink band wrapped around it. Got my daughter's name on it."

"Damn, in all this excitement, I forgot. Congratulations, Hammer. How's Maeve?"

"Just as perfect as her mini-me. By the way, she's with Pearl. Tell her I'll be right behind you if you beat me there."

Decker approached and handed me his key fob. "I'll get a ride back with Edge and Crash." He looked over to where Scottie waited with Pearl's mother. "You've got other business to take care of."

"There's still a lot to do here."

"We'll manage without you. Plus, I don't want Opal to see whatever we're about to find in there." He motioned with his head toward the compound. "Get along now."

"You aren't going to believe what Rage and I found!" shouted Ink, running back from the compound's gate.

"What?" Decker shouted back.

"It was a bloodbath, all right, but apparently, Scottie, with Ms. Opal's help, was able to get most if not all the women and children tucked away safely in an underground bunker."

I turned toward the two women Decker was already approaching. I couldn't hear what he said, but Scottie hugged him.

"I hope to hell he's offering her a job," muttered Vex.

"Yeah?"

"Hell, yeah."

"He is," said Fury, walking away.

"If the three of us are going to be a team, we're gonna have to take her down a peg."

I laughed. "I wish you a helluva lotta luck with that, Vex."

Hammer chuckled. "You got that right."

I left the two men to chat and joined Decker, who was talking to Ink and Rage.

"For tonight and maybe the next few days, the two of you will stay on the compound along with Jagger and Steel," I heard him say. "After the hotwash tomorrow, we'll assess the situation here and see what kind of resources are available to help these women. Ink, you're in charge."

"Roger that," he said.

Decker turned to me. "Pearl, Ms. Opal, and even Scottie may be able to help determine what kind of aid these women will need while we figure out their options."

"I can answer that in part. There are several cult-survivor support groups. Some provide only counseling, but others are set up to house families who have escaped cult life and get them reacclimated. That can include reconnecting them with family."

He raised a brow.

"I've done a lot of research on cult survivors, given the compound functioned as such."

"Good work, Rip." Decker turned back to Ink. "For tonight, get them settled and reassure them help is on the way."

"Sir, I'm not sure the women will be comfortable with me here," said Rage. As a black man, he brought up a good point.

"You're right. Ink, Rock will stay in Rage's place."

"Yes, sir."

"Rage, you'll work with Rip to help find resources and support for the families."

"We should also consider grief counseling, sir. Many lost their husbands and fathers."

"Another good point. Get that set up too."

"Yes, sir," he repeated.

"Carry on," Decker said, motioning for them to return to the compound. "You, head out," he said to me.

"Will do." Before I got too far from him, Decker called me back.

"How do you think Ms. Opal is going to feel about leaving the compound?"

"Probably similarly to how Pearl felt, but if she is her mother, my guess is she's equally resilient."

24

Pearl

When Angel came out from the back of the house without her computer, she was smiling.

"Rip wanted me to tell you he's on his way here now," she said, looking at me before turning to Maeve. "And that Hammer is right behind him."

"Thank God," I murmured at the same time I heard Maeve whisper, "Praise the Lord."

Angel walked over, knelt beside me, and took my hand in hers. "He also wanted me to tell you he's bringing someone very special with him."

"Ms. Opal?" I asked through my tears.

Angel's eyes teared up too. "Yes."

"Is she my mother?"

"She is."

I looked over at Maeve, who had tears running down her cheeks too. All three of us were smiling, though.

"You're going to meet your mum, Pearl. Wait, you already knew her, just not that she was Ms. Opal, or

Ms. Opal was her. Now I'm confusing even myself," said Maeve. "Oh! Wait! Pearl and Opal."

"Pearl and Opal," Angel repeated.

"My mother."

The only way I could sit still was if I held the baby. The entire time Maeve was feeding her, I paced in front of the window to the point where she demanded I be seated. As soon as I did, she handed Mary to me.

When I saw lights from the driveway and Angel announced Rip had returned, I handed Mary back and jumped up from the couch.

"We'll be in the other room," Angel said, leading Maeve into one of the bedrooms. I appreciated them respecting the privacy of what was about to happen and thanked her.

I watched as Rip helped Ms. Opal out of the SUV. It hadn't been that long since I last saw her on the compound, but she looked different, even from what little I could see in the dark.

What appeared the same, though, was the way her shoulders hunched forward and her gaze cast downward. So many of the women's bodies at the compound had the same stance. To me, it had always looked like defeat.

I opened the front door when they got close. "Please come in," I said in the same way I imagined Maeve would since she was the most gracious person I knew. "It's nice to see you, Ms. Opal," I added.

She peered up at me almost as if she was anticipating I'd be angry. I wasn't. Not even a little.

"I'm so glad you're here now and safe. I want you to know I understand everything that happened and why."

"Thank you," she said just above a whisper. She looked around. "Is this your house?"

"No. We're just staying here for now." I looked over at Rip. His expression was so full of love it nearly made my heart burst.

"Excuse me," I said to Ms. Opal and walked straight into his arms. "I'm so glad you're safe too," I said, hugging him as tightly as I could. "And thank you."

"You're welcome." He leaned down, and we kissed. "I'll get changed and give you two a chance to talk."

"I think Angel and Maeve are in one of the bedrooms."

He looked up when another vehicle pulled into the driveway. A third was right behind it. "That'll be

Hammer and Crash. I'll have them come in through the garage."

"It's okay, Rip. I'd like Ms. Opal to meet our friends. Can you please ask everyone to come out…or in?"

He smiled. "I will."

"I had a cup of chamomile tea earlier. Would you like one?" I asked when Rip left the room.

"I would, please."

I took her hand and led her over to the kitchen island. "Please have a seat."

She looked as uncomfortable as I remembered feeling the first night I stayed in Rip's house. Everything had been unfamiliar and me, so unsure of myself. I still felt that way, often actually, but I knew *our friends*, as I'd said to Rip, would welcome Ms. Opal—my mother—just like they had me.

Her eyes opened wide when I pressed the lever near the sink and steaming hot water flowed into the cup.

"If you think that's something, Rip's phone turns on all the lights in his house. Off too. It doesn't make coffee, though."

Maeve came out of the bedroom and introduced herself and baby Mary. "Is this Ms. Opal who taught you to make blueberry pancakes?"

My mama—best I started thinking of her that way, instead of Ms. Opal—looked at me. "Like she said, you taught me to make them, so that's what I wrote on the recipe for Maeve."

"They are my favorite. I fear my husband will grow tired of me asking him to make them every day."

"Your husband?"

"That's me," said Hammer, coming in from the garage. "We met at the compound."

"This is Angel," I said when the other woman came out of the bedroom. "Angel, I'd like you to meet Ms. Opal."

"Just Opal," she said, shaking Angel's hand.

Maeve handed the baby to Hammer and approached me. "We're leaving for the ranch now. If there's anything at all you need, just ask Rip to let us know."

"She can do it herself," he said, handing me a phone. "I've programmed as many numbers as I could think of into it."

My mama leaned close to me. "Does yours turn on the lights too?"

I looked at Rip, who chuckled. "I'll make sure to program that in too as soon as we get home. In fact, do you want to stay here tonight or there?"

"There, if you wouldn't mind." I knew my way around Rip's house a lot better than around the one we were in, although as late as it was, all we'd be doing was sleeping.

"I'd rather spend the night in my own bed, to be honest."

"My mama will need a few things, like I did when I first arrived," I whispered to him.

"All taken care of."

I didn't know how, but I was getting to know Rip, so that he'd made sure my mama had what she needed shouldn't come as a surprise.

It didn't take very long to get from the King-Alexander Ranch to the Hammered Dubliner, but my mother fell asleep in the backseat almost right away.

"It's been a long day for all of us, although probably longer for her," commented Rip.

"A long week. She said she hasn't slept very much since Mr. Robinson took me off the compound."

"I know the two of you didn't have a chance to talk."

"No, but the way I see it, we'll have all the time in the world now." Actually, I wondered if we did. Now that the ABT was pretty much gone, what would happen to us and the others who'd lived on the compound? I hadn't been off it long enough to have the slightest inkling of how to make my way in the world on my own. I had no idea whether my mother did, given she'd lived there almost all my life too.

"Pearl?"

I looked over at him.

"I can see your worry even in the dark."

"I can't help it. I asked before what would happen to me, but now it isn't just me. It's my mother too. And the other women and their children whose lives will be upended."

"Decker and I had a conversation about it before I left. He has four of our guys helping those remaining at the compound get settled. They're also assisting the other agencies by doing a sweep of the property and handling additional arrests. Tomorrow, we'll begin the process of helping the other women figure out their next steps."

"What does that mean?"

"Some may have families to return to. Some may not. There are national agencies who have resources to help."

"What if they want to stay?"

"I hadn't thought of that specifically, but I'm sure it is something that will be discussed. How much of a possibility do you think that will be?"

"The women do all the work anyway."

Rip chuckled. "Women rule the world, darlin', and I'm not being sarcastic when I say that."

"He's right," my mother said from the backseat. Either she woke up or hadn't been asleep, to begin with.

I looked over the seat at her. "Do you think many will want to stay?"

"There are some who will, just because it's the life they know. Others have been trying to leave the compound for months, if not longer. Pearl, you remember how many left after the FBI raid two years ago?"

It wasn't just women who had left, back then. Lots of men had too. We'd also heard many of those had been arrested and were either already in prison or in jail, awaiting trial.

Rip reached over and took my hand. "As far as you and your mother are concerned, your home is with me for as long as you want it to be."

Again, I didn't know what that meant, but I wouldn't ask now. It was after one in the morning, and we were all dead tired.

25

"How are Pearl and Opal getting on?" Maeve asked when I arrived at Hammer's the next morning for the hotwash.

"Opal is as tentative as Pearl was initially, but they're finding their way, slowly but surely."

"I'm so glad." There was a wail from a walkie-talkie-looking device that hung from Maeve's pocket. "I'm off. Miss Mary is hungry." She leaned up and kissed my cheek. "You're a good man, Rip. Pearl is a lucky woman." She walked away, but stopped and looked over her shoulder. "Do not let her get away."

"What did she say?" asked Hammer, coming to stand beside me.

"Not to let Pearl get away."

"Is she trying to?"

I shook my head and laughed. "Do we have a meeting this morning or not?"

"Nice subject change. And, yes. You're the first one here, other than Money."

"When did he get in? I didn't know he'd be here."

"Purely coincidental. He came to town to meet his niece. Now that he has, I'm not sure we'll ever get him to leave."

Once again, I had a hard time marrying the image of the man I knew with a doting uncle, but after seeing how he was with his sister, I shouldn't.

"He's in here."

Hammer led me into the main dining room, where Money was studying something on his computer.

"Rip, I'll be right with you," he said without looking up.

"Yes, sir."

"Have a seat," said Hammer, motioning to the chair at the head of the table. I pulled out the one beside it and set my computer down.

"Not there." He pointed. *"There."*

"Okay, okay." I shifted my computer over.

Decker arrived shortly after. I was glad since being the only person besides Money at the table and with an open seat between us, I was feeling mighty awkward. However, the one time I thought about switching places, Hammer glared at me as if he was reading my mind.

Decker pulled out the chair on the opposite side of Money, leaving me feeling just as uncomfortable. "Any update?" he asked.

"Nothing confirmed."

Decker looked at me. "You ready for this?"

"Yes, sir." I'd gotten up before sunrise to prepare my report and was glad I had since, as soon as I finished, Pearl joined me in the kitchen. It felt so good to be able to sit and chat with her over breakfast, like we'd gotten used to doing. By the time I left, Opal had just woken up and joined us.

Within the next few minutes, those who'd been at the compound the night before filed into the room. Decker motioned for Fury to sit on one side of me and Vex on the other. Ink, Rage, Shredder, Steel, Edge, and Rock took random seats. As they did, I nodded in their direction.

"You ready?" Decker asked Money.

"Go ahead."

Deck shrugged and stood. "As we all know, most of the Aryan Brotherhood of Texas was wiped out last night prior to our team's arrival. We didn't have to lift much of a finger. The two sides practically annihilated each other. What we know now is how it started." He turned to Shredder. "You're up."

Shredder stood. "Yesterday at twelve hundred hours, Luke Howell received word that Pearl had paid a visit to John Clinton at the Supermax prison in Florence. He was also briefed on who was at the prison with her."

"The guards," I mumbled. "That's why he wouldn't talk." Which meant that him asking Pearl whether she still had the teddy bear was the accelerent to the firestorm already smoldering on the compound.

Shredder's gaze met mine. "Yes, sir. Howell had more contacts inside the prison, who also confirmed that an attorney and 'another man' accompanied Pearl."

"Which meant he figured out she wasn't in Idaho. Probably that she never had been."

"Affirmative," said Shredder.

Money looked up from his computer. "I can confirm inmate John Clinton was found unresponsive in his cell yesterday at twenty hundred hours. He was pronounced dead shortly after."

That explained why Money had remained so intent on his computer. He was waiting for that confirmation. Twenty hundred hours was also when Vex messaged that all hell was breaking loose at the compound.

"Go on," Money said to Shredder.

"I was able to get word to Scottie, who along with Ms. Opal's help, got the women and children into the underground bunker before the battle began."

"That was the reason I couldn't get her off the compound," said Vex.

"Where is Scottie?" I asked.

"She was summoned by DHS," Vex muttered. "She gave me her report."

"We know what the trigger was, but why the war?" I asked.

"There were two splinters," answered Decker. "One at the Nation, and one at the ABT. What they were looking for was dirt on the council of three to stage their coup. I can confirm there were mounds of it. Not just on them, though. However, those three are looking at significant prison time, as are many other members of the Nation."

"How did they know there was any?" I asked.

"This is conjecture," said Vex. "But Howell took over Fischer's quarters. My guess is he stumbled onto something that made him think Clinton had gathered it," said Vex.

"I think I know how," said Shredder. "He found a photo."

"Of?" I asked.

"The only person recognizable in it was Clinton, but he was with a woman holding a baby. You can't see the woman's face, but it gave Howell the idea that maybe the baby was Pearl."

"That's why he arranged for her to have a DNA test."

Shredder looked at me and nodded. "From what I could glean, the results came back the same day Vex took Pearl off the compound."

"What happened to the photo?" I asked.

Shredder shrugged. "No idea. I only saw it one time, and even then, I didn't get a good look at it. Maybe he destroyed it."

"How did he know Clinton had evidence against the council of three?"

"There were rumors about why the guy was never killed in prison."

The weight of what Pearl's father did when we visited him was immediately apparent. "Right. That's how he stayed alive all these years. Edwards, Miller, and Pezak knew he had evidence against them, but not where until he asked Pearl about her bear. He had to know that meant his days were numbered," I said.

"He was dying anyway," said Money. "Had less than six months to live, according to prison records. Terminal cancer."

"What went down up in Idaho?" Decker asked Money, grinning.

"The men Rip mentioned, aka the council of three, were apprehended while fleeing the compound. We had enough people on the inside that it didn't turn into a war like it did with the ABT. Just a massive raid."

"Was there anyone who wasn't arrested?" Decker asked.

"Outside of our agents? Negative."

"That's what I like to hear." He rubbed his hands together and looked over at Hammer. "Where the hell are those stogies?"

Hammer shook his head. "Not in the house, Deck. Maeve and the baby are upstairs."

"As far as what happened at the ABT compound, Howell figured that since Clinton told Pearl about the teddy bear, he'd what? Take control by force?" I asked.

"That's right. He knew he'd lost his leverage, so he made the call to proceed," said Shredder.

"Except the major and I had already planted the seeds of a potential uprising with the original ABTers," said Vex. "When the splinters fired the first shot and the original group fired back, Howell knew his only chance at getting out of there alive was to get his hands on Scottie, Opal, and me. Take you and Decker out too." He looked at me before readdressing Shredder. "You, though, blindsided him."

Shredder smiled. "You eluded them too."

"I saw them nab Scottie and Opal but knew I was vastly outnumbered. I can't tell you how happy I was to see all of you arrive."

"Did the major make it out?" I asked.

Vex shook his head. "He was among the first down."

I hated to hear it. It always hit hard when we lost one of the good guys.

I studied Vex. The man looked like he could use a solid month of R and R. I hoped the Invincibles were prepared to give it to him. He'd certainly earned it.

"Anything we missed?" Decker asked, looking around the table.

Ink raised his hand.

"Go ahead," Decker told him.

"There are a total of eighteen women left on the compound and about double that number of children. According to the one who appears to be their chosen spokesperson, they had some idea significant trouble was brewing. In the last couple of days, a few had already left. Most who did had somewhere to go, meaning family."

"Pearl, Opal, and I had a conversation on our way to my place last night about whether there was any possibility for those who wanted to, to remain on the compound."

"Good question," said Decker. "I'll look into who owns the property. There's also the matter of how they'll support themselves. However, we won't address that now." Decker looked around the table. "Anything else?"

When no one else spoke up, Edge stood. "First, I want to apologize to Rip. This was his mission, and I went against direct orders to relinquish it. Those came from you, Money, when you handed the reins to Rip. While I'll apologize for the disrespect and not following orders, I stand by my decision to go into the compound myself. I should've finished this thing two years ago. I failed."

Money studied him but didn't say anything, so I did. "Apology accepted."

Edge nodded and took a seat.

As far as him feeling as though he'd failed, the raid two years ago had been conducted by the FBI with help from the CIA and the Invincibles team. Everyone believed it would be the end of the ABT, but they'd reorganized and come back with a vengeance no one anticipated.

Decker leaned back in his chair. "Next?" He looked at Money. "Do you want to lead, or should I?"

"Go ahead. This has nothing to do with me. At least directly."

Decker looked around the table. "Everybody but Rip, Vex, and Fury can clear out. Good work on this one, team. I hear there's a big celebration in the works over at the Long Branch. We'll keep you posted on when that will be."

Decker waited until everyone was gone but the three of us, Edge, Hammer, and Money before sitting back down at the table. "Rip, Fury, and Vex, last night, we talked about a new team. While Fury didn't hesitate to confirm she already knew about it"—Decker winked at her—"the two of you may not have realized we were serious."

Vex and I looked at one another.

"Edge and I represent the four original Invincibles partners, since Rile and Grinder are based in Europe and unable to be here today, in announcing our own 'splinter' group. This one is sanctioned, though. Right, Hammer?"

"That's right. I had Rile's and Grinder's proxy, so it's official."

Fury opened an envelope that sat on the table in front of her and pulled out two sets of documents. She handed one to me and one to Vex.

"You fellas look that proposal over, and when you're ready to talk, together or individually, Edge, Hammer, and I will make ourselves available. Fury has already had a chance to review her copy, and we've come to an official agreement."

I read the top two lines. "This says partnership."

Decker smiled and nodded. "That's right. I'd say the three of you have earned it."

"So what's this about a big celebration?" I asked after skimming the first page and realizing my brain wasn't ready to process the contents of the contract.

"Should we tell him or keep it a surprise?" Hammer asked Decker.

"We better tell him, or he might not show up."

"Buck gave me a call earlier this morning and said you missed out on seeing CB Rice when you were at the Roaring Fork. He reminded me that the band had never played at the Long Branch and suggested I book them."

"Yeah?" I had to admit, I felt as exhausted as Vex looked, but hearing CB Rice was coming to town perked me right up.

"What we're trying to work out is for them to be performing here this Sunday night. Maeve and I have agreed to close the Long Branch for a private party. Oh, and Rebel wanted me to tell you she'd be sure to have catfish on the menu."

"That sounds damned good, Hammer. Thank you."

"I'm hoping Uncle Kellen is willing to stick around until then, so he can babysit Mary."

Money shook his head and laughed. "My niece will probably be more fun than all of you combined."

When Decker stood, Fury, Vex, and I did too.

"I'll be in touch," I told him when he walked me to the door.

"I'll look forward to it. Oh, and be sure to read the start date along with the section on vacation time." He winked.

"Yes, sir."

26

Pearl

I couldn't explain why I felt so nervous when Rip left shortly after my mother joined us in the kitchen. I had so many questions, and some, I wasn't sure I wanted answers to.

"Can I get you some coffee or tea?" I asked.

"Coffee, if it's made."

I glanced over and noticed she was wringing her hands. "Look, you and I both know what we have to talk about isn't going to be easy. I say we agree now to be understanding and forgiving, knowing how hard some of the decisions we made were."

When I set her coffee on the table, she looked up and smiled. "You are generous in including yourself, Pearl. None of the decisions—good or bad—were yours. I have nothing to forgive you for."

"I'm sure I wasn't always a very nice person."

She shook her head. "There wasn't a day that passed when I wasn't proud of you. I knew you were meant for more than life with the ABT. However, your father and my brother did everything in their power to protect us as best as they could.”

“I understand that. Truly. And my dad—uncle— treated me decently. He did protect me.”

She laughed. “It was that, or he knew he’d be in big trouble with me.” Her expression changed. “Don’t think he was a good man, though, Pearl. He may have been to you, and to me, at least to a certain extent, but for that, he was rewarded handsomely.”

“What does that mean?”

“Financially. Not that he could flaunt it or even use much of it. I think he was biding his time, though. Once Clinton died, I think John intended to figure out a way to get you and me off the compound.”

“I never saw the two of you interact much. Not at all, actually.”

“We couldn’t. It was too much of a risk.”

“Were you close?”

She laughed. “Not at all. I was older than him, and he’d always been a damn rebel. Got mixed up with the wrong crowd from way back. Not that I was a saint.” She winked. “I could blame your father for that, but I wasn’t completely innocent.” She studied me. “You probably don't even think of him that way. Or of me as your mother."

I took a deep breath and let it out slowly, giving myself time to think through what I wanted to say. "Even before I knew, I remembered you were always nice to me. Most of the other women on the compound weren't. Last night, when I realized that out of everyone there, you had to be my mother, I guess I started thinking of you that way."

Her eyes filled with tears. "If anyone ever found out who you really were…"

"I think they did. That man—Howell, I think was his name—did a DNA test on me a few weeks back. I only know that because I had another one a few days ago. Anyway, that's why Mr. Robinson took me off the compound. Ms. Shay overheard Howell saying he was going to use me to get what he wanted from the Aryan Nation."

"I'd already decided to tell him and his bunch that I had been Clinton's woman and I'd give them what they wanted as long as they didn't lay a hand on you. Before I could, someone told me Mr. Robinson left for Idaho with you and his woman."

"They aren't who everyone thought they were."

She nodded. "Figured that out last night."

"Did you know what was in the bear?"

This time, she shook her head. "Not exactly, just that whatever it was, was 'insurance.'"

"How did Howell know?"

"Your uncle kept one photo of your father, me, and you when you were a baby. I had no idea he even had it. I don't know why he did. Maybe somewhere deep in his soul, he planned to tell you who you really were. Then again, maybe he thought he could use it to get even more money."

"How did you find out about it?"

She reached inside her shirt and pulled something out. "I saw it sticking out of Howell's pocket last night when he was holding me with a gun to my head. After he was shot, I grabbed it when no one was looking." She handed it to me.

"You can't see your face."

"I guess that was the only thing that saved my life. Yours too."

Seeing the photo affected me much more than I'd expected it to. While we were never a family, I had parents who loved me enough to make sacrifices in their lives to protect me. My mother had lived and worked beside me all my life and never let on because her doing so would've jeopardized my safety. She hadn't been able to hug me or even be overly nice to me since it would've raised suspicion.

"There's something I need to ask you, and I want you to know that whatever your answer is, I won't be upset."

"Go ahead."

"Would you be okay with it if I called you Mama?"

She took my hands in hers, and when her eyes met mine, I knew what her answer would be. "I've waited all my life to hear you call me that."

"I know you love me, Mama. I know you always have."

27

Rip

When I came inside the house, I found Pearl and her mother in the kitchen, hugging. Both women were crying. I tried to back away and not intrude, but Pearl opened her eyes and looked into mine.

She eased away from Opal and walked straight to me.

"Thank you," she said, hugging me tightly.

I stroked her hair with one hand and wrapped the other around her waist. "You have nothing to thank me for, darlin'."

Pearl looked up at me. "I have everything to thank you for. *Everything*." She took a step back and turned around. "Where did my mama go?"

"I think she wanted to give us some privacy. I take it this morning went okay?"

"We had a good talk, and I learned so much. I also asked her if I could call her that—Mama."

"I also take it she said you could."

Pearl smiled and nodded. "Oh, and look." She held out a photo.

"Shredder mentioned this earlier. Where did you get it?"

"My mama said she took it off Howell's body after he was shot."

I studied the image that had set a series of events in motion that led to Pearl and I being in each other's arms. I hated the danger she'd faced, but I'd forever look at the photo as what brought us together. No matter what happened next, I'd love her. I knew that in my heart. Even if that meant I'd have to let her go, give her the freedom to live the way she wanted to, for the first time in her life.

"My guess is you want to spend some more time with your mother. I have a few things to take care of at the barn, so I'll head out now and leave you two be."

"Are you going to ride out?"

"Probably. It's been a few days since I have."

"Can I go with you?"

I smiled. "Of course you can. You *always* can. I just thought—"

"Do you promise?"

"What do you mean?"

"Do you promise that I can always ride out with you? Every day. Forever and ever."

"Forever and ever. As long as *you* want to."

"You keep saying that. Do you think there'll come a time I don't? Or don't want to stay here with you? You said that last night."

I took her hands in mine and stroked the back of them with my thumbs. "There is a whole wide world open to you now, Pearl. I would like nothing better than to be the man who shows you that world, but I also want you to know you're free to explore it with me or without me."

My heart nearly broke when her eyes filled with tears. "Why are you crying?"

"I can't imagine wanting to without you, Rip. I don't want to without you."

I looked up at the ceiling and closed my eyes. "You can't know that, Pearl."

"Look at me."

I lowered my head.

"You say I can stay with you as long as I want to. You say you want to be the man who shows me the whole wide world. How can you know that's what you want when, at the same time, you say I can't know it too? That doesn't seem fair to me. You don't know your mind any better than I know mine. You don't know your heart better than I know mine, either."

"You don't know how much I wish—"

She stepped back and put her hands on her hips. "Stop saying 'you don't know.' *I know*. I know how I feel, and I know I love you, Rip. Can you say the same thing?"

"Yes."

She dropped her hands. "What?"

"I said *yes*. Yes, I can say the same thing. Yes, I love you."

"Are you *sure*?" she said, smirking.

"Get back over here, woman." I pulled her into my arms. "Yes, I'm sure."

She reached up and cupped my cheek with her palm. "Make me your woman, Rip. Claim me as yours and never let me go."

"How about if we claim each other, Pearl? You be mine, and I'll be yours."

"Forever and ever."

"That's right, darlin'. Forever and ever." I kissed her. "You know, I'm thinking maybe I'll skip going to the barns today."

"What are you going to do instead?"

"How would you like to see if your mama is as good at fishing as you are?"

Pearl and Opal packed us a picnic lunch before we left to spend the afternoon at the lake. Once we arrived, I told her there was something I wanted to show them both before I got the fishing tackle out of the truck.

I grabbed the rolled-up paper I had in the backseat and led them over to one of the markers I'd stuck in the ground a few months back. I unrolled the paper and asked Pearl to hold one side of it while I held the other.

"This is where the front door would be," I said, tapping the stake with my foot and pointing at the house plans we were holding. From there, I walked us over to where I intended the kitchen to be, then the living room and dining room. "What do you think?" I asked Pearl.

"You would live here instead of at the ranch?"

"*We* would live here." I looked from Pearl over to Opal. "All three of us. This plan is for five bedrooms, but we could always add more if we need them."

Pearl's eyes opened wide. "*Five* bedrooms? Your house on the ranch only has three."

"See? Not big enough for all of us to live in. Plus, I'm sure my mama and dad will want to come visit too. Especially when they have grandkids to spoil." I leaned closer to Pearl. "Remember, you said forever and ever. We need a home of our own to spend all those years in," I whispered.

She turned her head and kissed me. "I love you, Rip."

"I love you, Pearl."

"What do you think, Mama?"

Opal's eyes were full of tears, and she had her hands clasped near her face. "I think this is a dream come true. It's almost too good to be real."

"You ready to catch some fish?" I asked.

"You know how to fish?" Opal asked Pearl.

"Sure do. In fact, better than he does."

For the next six nights, Pearl and I kissed outside her door and said good night before sleeping in separate bedrooms. I know that if I asked, she would've joined me in mine, but it didn't feel right. Maybe I was setting myself up for the impossible, but I wanted the first time Pearl and I were together intimately to be so much more than just the first time she had sex. I wanted it to be romantic, special, not just for her, but for both of us.

I couldn't see a way to make it happen by me sweeping her off her feet to the other side of my house at the ranch, where her newly found mother slept in one of the other bedrooms.

I also didn't feel comfortable leaving Opal alone at the house and taking Pearl to a hotel somewhere.

Sunday afternoon, Opal pulled me aside, saying she'd volunteered to stay with baby Mary after Maeve called Pearl to say Money had been summoned back to Washington, DC, so she wouldn't be able to be at the Long Branch for the party.

"I made arrangements to stay at Maeve and Hammer's tonight so y'all didn't feel like you had to be back by any certain time. I appreciate all you've done, how much you and Pearl have included me in everything, but I think it's best for you to have a night to yourselves."

After thanking her, I told Pearl I had a few things to take care of and went to use my office down at the barns.

"You're goin' to the Branch tonight, right?" Pete asked.

"You know it."

"I was sorry to hear Ms. Opal won't be there." Pete and Opal had met when Pearl and I came down to ride out, and she'd begged off, saying she'd rather hang out at the barn. After she did the same thing the next day and the day after that, I realized she and Pete might be getting a little sweet on each other.

"You know she's babysitting?"

Pete kicked at the dirt. "Yeah, I do."

"I know you don't want to miss going to the Branch, but she might like some company, if you're so inclined."

"You don't think Hammer would mind?"

"Mind what?" the man asked, walking into my office.

"Pete was just saying it was a shame Ms. Opal would be all on her own tonight."

Hammer took the stogie I'd never seen him light out of his mouth and smiled. "Is that right?"

"He was wonderin' if you'd mind him paying her a visit."

"Of course I don't mind." Hammer chuckled. "Maeve is gonna love this." He turned to walk out.

"Where are you goin'?"

"Hell, I forgot why I came down here. I went by the house, and Pearl said you were here. Have you had a chance to review the contract Decker gave you?"

I led him out of the barn. "Yeah, it's very generous. I'm just not sure…"

"About what?"

"The truth is, I'm not sure I'd have time to handle my duties on the Hammered Dubliner."

He smiled. "I love that name more and more every time I hear it."

I laughed. "Is that all you've got to say?"

"Listen, you and I both know your time here was only temporary. And by here, I mean managing the ranch. The house you live in is yours. I hope you know that."

I kicked at the dirt like Pete had a few minutes ago. "About that."

Hammer laughed again. "Yeah?"

"I'm about to break ground on the place at Lady Bird Lake. The contractor says he thinks it'll be ready to move into in about six months."

Hammer patted my back. "I'm damn glad to hear it, Rip. I mean that sincerely." He raised a brow and studied me. "You got anything else you're ready to announce?"

I shook my head and chuckled. "Not yet."

"But soon, right?"

I rolled my eyes. "Yes, boss."

"Cuz Maeve and I were just discussing what a nice place our house is for a wedding."

"I'm sure it is. I'm still sorry I missed the other one." I'd been in the thick of things with the ABT mission when Hammer and Maeve were married.

"So, the contract?"

"Yeah?"

"You gonna sign it?"

"I think I am."

"Good. Decker said Vex signed two days ago. He was hoping we'd be able to celebrate the new team tonight. You were the only holdout. I'll tell him the party can proceed. You got a name?"

"I haven't even signed the contract yet."

"Well, best get started on that, unless you want to be called the Invincibles Part Two."

"Definitely not."

"Let's see, you're signing the contract, you're breaking ground on your house. Seems like there's one more thing we should be celebrating tonight."

"*Stop it.* I mean it."

"Maeve warned you not to let her get away."

"You can assure her I have no intention of doing so, and neither does Pearl."

"Then, I say it's time you make it official. You don't want to waste all that extra R & R Decker had Fury work into your contract when you could be spending it on a honeymoon."

I laughed again. "For God's sake, Hammer. Quit it."

"All right, all right, I'll lay off now. Maeve made me promise to try. I gave it my best shot," he said as he walked away.

I wasn't sure what Maeve had made him promise to try, but I wasn't about to reopen the conversation by asking. Plus, I came down here for a reason. I had a special night to plan and not much time to do it in.

28

Pearl

"Hammer said Pete called to tell him Rip was down at the barns," said Maeve when I opened the door and saw her standing there with Mary in her arms. "Hurry, we don't have much time."

"For what?" I asked, motioning her to come in.

"To decide what you're going to wear tonight." Maeve walked over to my mother. "Hello, Opal. You wouldn't mind taking Mary for a minute, would you?"

"You never have to ask. Come to Grandma Opal," said my mama, holding her arms out to take the baby.

"I brought several dresses for you to choose from. They're in the car. I'll go get them."

"Several?" I said, following her outside.

"Rip's favorite color is blue," she said as she held up dress after blue dress.

"I guess that's obvious."

"This one is by far the sexiest. I think you should try it on first."

I had to admit, I was a little frustrated each night when Rip walked me to my bedroom door and kissed me good night. Maybe between my mama staying at the house with Mary and me wearing a sexy dress, we wouldn't sleep in separate beds when we got home. However, the one she held up did not look like it would fit me, and I said so.

"Just try it on," Maeve insisted.

When I did, I couldn't believe how well it fit or how sexy it looked. It went over one shoulder but in the back, had three straps. The skirt fell just above my knees and had a ruffled hem.

"Come out and let us see," said Maeve, knocking on the bedroom door.

I slid my feet into the matching high-heeled shoes she also brought and opened the door.

"It's *perfect*!" she gasped. "Okay, change back into your other clothes and come with me."

"Where are we going?"

"You, Grandma Opal, Mary, and I are going up to the house to get ready. Rip will pick you up there."

"Why?"

"Because you're going on a date," my mama said.

29

Rip

I'd just hung up from making reservations when my cell rang with a call from Hammer.

"What now?" I answered.

Hammer laughed. "Maeve says you're to pick Pearl up at our place at seven on the dot."

"At your place?"

"Yeah, you know, like a date. Oh, and you're to bring flowers."

"Flowers? What kind of flowers?"

"You're hopeless."

"Okay, I'm hopeless. That doesn't tell me what kind of flowers I'm supposed to bring."

"Romantic ones." Hammer ended the call.

"Romantic flowers? What the hell does that mean?" I muttered to myself.

"Roses are romantic," said Pete from just outside my office door. "Red ones."

It wasn't like this was the first date I'd ever gone on. Not even close. But it sure as hell felt like it, and that was without anyone knowing what I had planned for later when Pearl and I left the Long Branch.

"Red roses, you say?"

I got up, shooed Pete away from the door, and shut it before calling back the hotel concierge I'd just spoken to. Maeve might give me shit for not following her instructions, but little did she know I'd be doing her one far better.

I checked the time and saw I had a little over an hour to return to the house, shower, change, and pack a bag for me and one for Pearl before it was time for me to leave.

I tried on four different pearl-snaps before settling on the one I thought she'd like the most. I pulled on my perfectly pressed jeans and best cowboy boots before grabbing my sport coat and hat and heading out the door.

As I was climbing into my SUV, I noticed a patch of blue off in the distance. It was early for my favorite flower to bloom, and they weren't red roses, but I'd taken care of that for later, so I walked over and picked a handful of bluebonnets.

When I drove up to the house, I saw Hammer sitting out on the deck, waiting for me.

"Hi, Mr. Anderson, I'm here to pick up Pearl for our prom date."

Hammer laughed. "I was told to wait outside. Apparently, we're double-dating. By the way, nice flowers," he said, eyeing the stems I was clutching.

"We need to go in separate cars."

"Good, because Maeve and I are riding in the Porsche."

"Which one?" I asked, looking over at the identical set sitting in the driveway.

"Hers." Hammer motioned me to the front door, where he stopped and knocked.

The Long Branch was my favorite bar, and CB Rice was my favorite band, but tonight I didn't care about either. All I could think about was the woman in my arms. The music of Pearl's laughter drowned that of the band, and her smile eclipsed the stage lights.

Her breathy moans when she took her first bite of T-bone steak fresh off the grill turned my cock rock-hard, just like they had the first night when she first tasted the burger from the drive-through and when her eyes rolled back in her head when she tried the twice-baked potato. All I could think about was how I wanted them to do exactly that as I thrust into her hot, wet pussy again and again.

The dress she wore was the sexiest fucking thing I'd ever seen. Its color matched the bouquet of bluebonnets I'd given her when Opal opened the door to let Hammer and me into his house.

As we danced, I wrapped my arm around her waist, wishing I could sink my teeth into her bare shoulder and slide my hand under the short skirt to first grip the firm cheeks of her ass before fingering the wetness I knew I'd find between her legs.

I groaned in frustration at the fantasies I couldn't stop from playing on repeat, counting the minutes until I decided it was late enough for us to leave without seeming rude.

While the others who'd been part of the ABT mission indulged in heavy pours of beer and several rounds of shots, I abstained from it, not wanting to cloud my memories of the night ahead with alcohol.

"Are you okay?" Pearl asked as I heard yet another groan escape my own lips.

"I'm not."

She pulled back to look at me. "What's wrong?"

"I want to be alone with you. I need to be alone with you," I practically growled.

Pearl's pupils dilated, and her breath caught. "I want the same thing."

"Think it's too early for us to leave?"

She studied me. "I don't care what anyone thinks, Rip. Five minutes after we got here wouldn't have been too early for me."

I knew that didn't mean she wasn't having fun. Her need for me was as great as mine was for her.

"Let's go." I took her hand and led her to the door, praying no one stopped us on our way out. When we got to the SUV without being waylaid, I breathed a sigh of relief.

"Kiss me," she said when I opened the passenger door. I dropped my mouth to hers, taking my time, showing her exactly how a man kissed a woman he desperately wanted to make love to. Slowly, deliberately, I swiped my tongue over hers before trailing my lips from her mouth to her neck.

When my name escaped her lips, more of a moan or a cry, I cupped her ass with one hand. "This dress… you…your smell…your taste…your everything. God, Pearl, do you know how much I want you?"

Her fingers dug into the flesh of my arms. "Please," she whispered.

"Do you want me too, Pearl? Do you want me to show you how much pleasure I can give you?"

"Please," she repeated in a throaty moan this time.

As difficult as it was to stop touching her, I'd made plans. Plans for Pearl, so our first time together was as special as I could possibly make it. "Get in the truck, darlin'."

The drive from the Long Branch to the hotel where I'd made reservations seemed to take forever, yet once we arrived, all I could remember was the way Pearl looked in the seat beside me. Her pouty lips were swollen from my kisses, and her eyes were heavy with lust. Only once did I reach over and put my hand on her leg, instantly removing it when I knew, if I didn't, I'd slide my fingers between her legs like I'd wanted to when we were dancing.

I stopped at the self-check-in, slid my credit card in the reader, and grabbed the key card that popped out of the machine. I took Pearl's hand in mine and led her to the bank of elevators, and pressed the key card against the pad until the light flashed green and we started to move. The doors opened directly into the suite I'd reserved. I looked down at the trail of rose petals I'd requested run from there to where their redness was scattered on the bed.

"Tell me you want this, Pearl. Tell me you understand what's about to happen between us."

"I do," she answered, barely above a whisper, not because she was afraid, but because she was as breathless with desire as I was.

"The first thing we're going to do is undress each other." When she nodded, her eyes wide, I knew I'd just lied. Before anything else, I had to kiss her again.

I wove my fingers into her hair and angled her head where I wanted it. Her lips parted, and she swiped her tongue against mine as though she was begging me to take her to that place no man ever had before. I intended to, and so much farther beyond that. By the time the sun rose in the morning, I vowed Pearl would experience pleasure like she'd never dreamed existed. I would taste every inch of her bare skin, marking her as mine with every lick.

"Do you feel how hard you make me?" I said when she ground her body against mine.

Every plan I'd made to take this slow, reveling in her innocence and purity, was lost. I unfastened the clasp that held her dress together and nearly knelt at her feet when it slid from her body, revealing its nakedness beneath it. My God, all night, she'd been pantyless, and I hadn't known it. We wouldn't even have made it inside the bar if I had.

"Leave them on," I demanded when I saw her about to remove the sexy stilettos she wore. "I've had fantasies all night about seeing you in nothing but them."

I lifted her in my arms and rested her body on the soft rose petals scattered on the bed.

I toed off my boots, and with one hand, I released the snaps on my shirt, not caring if I tore it from my body. Pearl watched me undress, her eyes wide when I opened my pants and my cock spilled free. Her cheeks flamed, and she gasped as her gaze took in the size of me, making me smile.

Once I was naked and all that remained on her were the sexy heels, I climbed on the bed, thrust my hands beneath her bottom, and lifted her to my mouth.

A soft moan spilled from her lips as I gently stroked her folds with my tongue. Her sweetness coated my lips as I swirled her clit with my tongue before my mouth dipped lower, making her shudder. I teased her, bringing her to the edge again and again, then slowing only to speed up again when I felt her tension ease.

She was trembling when I lowered her bottom and knelt between her legs. Unable to resist, I swiped her clit with my thumb, loving the way her mouth opened and soft moans spilled from somewhere deep inside her.

I slid one finger into her heat and leaned over to kiss her. I was tempted to add a second, to continue driving her wild with just my hands and mouth, but I knew my entering her for the first time would be easier if she was drenched and on the edge of climaxing.

I stayed on my knees between her spread legs and sheathed myself with the condom I'd tossed on the bed before removing my jeans.

I inserted just the tip of my cock into her heat, and Pearl whimpered. I looked into her eyes. "This may hurt, my love. But only for a minute, then it will feel like heaven."

She nodded, her eyes never leaving mine as I reached up and cupped her cheek with one hand and held her hip with the other, slowly easing deeper into her tightness.

Finally knowing it was time, I thrust once and stilled, giving her a moment to recover from the shock of feeling me buried so deep. I pulled out slowly, seeing the proof of her innocence against the same color as the rose petals. The sight stirred something deep within me, and I lost myself in the feel of her squeezing me like a vise. I kept my eyes latched to hers, watching as they rolled back just like I'd hoped they would, and my name, screamed from her lips as her nails dug into my flesh, brought me to my own release.

As gingerly as I could, I eased myself from her body and removed the condom before tossing it in the trash. I lay beside Pearl and gathered her in my arms.

"I hope I didn't hurt you too much." I cringed, realizing I sounded like the most unromantic man alive as soon as I heard my own words spill from my lips.

"Hurt? No, Rip. You did not hurt me." She opened her eyes and looked over at the table by the bed, where another condom packet sat. "I want to know how it feels without one of those."

"You could get pregnant."

"I don't care. Do you? You claimed me, and I claimed you. If a baby comes of that, wouldn't it be the greatest expression of our love?"

"It would be."

"Plus, how else are we going to fill all the bedrooms in our new house?"

By the time the sun came up, Pearl and I had pleasured one another's bodies in every way I'd imagined and I knew I never wanted to spend another day without her by my side.

"Marry me, Pearl," I blurted. "I want you to be my wife and me to be your husband. Legally binding."

She smiled. "Forever and ever."

"That's right. Forever and ever."

Epilogue

Pearl
Six months later

"Are your eyes still closed?" Rip said when he parked the SUV.

"They are, but I'll remind you, I saw this house just last week."

"Humor him, sweetheart," my mother said from the backseat.

"Stay where you are. Do not move, and do not open your eyes."

"Yes, husband." As if I would. I loved it when he opened my door and held out his hand to help me out, especially now that a baby was growing inside me.

"Keep them closed," he warned as he led me by one hand while my mama put her arm through my free one. We came to a stop when I knew we had to be near the front door, and I waited while he opened it.

"Take a step up," he said. "Okay, you can open them."

When I did, the first thing I saw were red rose petals running from the front door, across the entryway, over to the staircase, and up, farther than I could see.

"Wait," he said when I went to step over the threshold. "I'm supposed to carry you."

I heard my mother giggle. "Don't drop her."

"I never would."

While I expected him to set me on my feet once we were inside, he kept going, all the way up the stairs. When we reached the top, I saw two trails of petals. The red ones led into the room I knew was ours. The others were pink and led to the room we'd decided would be for the baby.

"Want to see it?" he asked with the hopeful look he got that I found so sweet. Rip never needed to ask; I'd always want to see whatever he wanted to show me.

"Of course."

He didn't put me down until we entered the room that had been empty when I last saw it. Now, it was filled with the most beautiful crib I'd ever seen and a matching dresser. Near it, sat a rocker. I recognized the fabric on the cushions and knew my mama had sewn the covers as well as the skirt on the bottom of the crib and the curtains on the window. We'd picked it out together, and it was covered with baby angels—cherubs Maeve had called them—all wearing strands of pearls.

I walked over to the crib and ran my hand over the soft sheets in the room that looked out over the lake just like our bedroom did. I turned to my mother, who stood in the doorway.

"I love it," I said, looking from her to my husband.

In the days after he'd rescued my mother from the ABT compound, Rip believed I'd want to experience life on my own, know how it felt to be free, but what he thought would give me that, never would've. Only his love could. He opened my heart, and because he did, I was free to love, to learn, to experience everything there was in life, things I'd never dreamed existed.

I rested my hand where our baby grew. "She loves it too," I said, looking into Rip's eyes. "And she loves you just as much as I do."

He beamed like he so often did when we talked about our baby girl. He and Hammer were two peas in a pod that way. Both men loved that their firstborn children were girls.

Maeve and I weren't much different in being so happy that our daughters would become best friends just like she and I were. We vowed we'd see each other just as often even after we moved to the lake house full-time this week. Plus, with my mama helping Maeve as Mary's nanny part-time, I had reason to ride along with her when she drove to the ranch three days a week.

I could drive myself, too, whenever I felt like it since Rip had taught me to drive at the same time my mother had learned. He'd even gotten each of us our own car.

When she wasn't with me or Maeve and Mary, my mama spent time on the compound. She owned the land now. It's what she used the money she'd inherited from her brother for.

At first, she was worried she'd have to explain where my uncle had gotten it, but after she told Decker Ashford she wanted to use it to establish a trust that would see the women and children would always be cared for, even after she passed on, he assured her there was no money trail to prevent her from using her inheritance any way she saw fit. I couldn't help but wonder if that was true or if he'd made sure whatever trail there was had disappeared.

With Fury's guidance, she also helped some of the women set up businesses that would allow them to earn money of their own. There was a farm stand near the entrance to the compound that sold the extra produce they grew, plus jams and baked goods. There was talk they might expand to a regular store so they could offer clothing and crafts too.

Rip and Hammer had donated a few heads of cattle so they could have a cow-calf operation, then Rip had taught them and some of the older children how to manage it properly, unlike the one that had been there before.

My mama mentioned one more idea she had, and that was to start a catering business since they already had a commercial kitchen set up on the property. When Maeve heard her talking about it, she said she'd help out any way she could and suggested the perfect name would be *Opal's Fine Foods*.

There were days I felt like I didn't contribute much, but I was working on that. Shortly after Rip and I got married—almost five months ago to the day—we rode out like we usually did after breakfast and he asked me about my life's dreams.

I'd already been thinking about it, so I'd answered right away that I wanted to go to college. Since I'd been homeschooled at the compound, the first thing I had to do was get my high school GED. As soon as I had, I enrolled at the local community college but planned to transfer to the University of Texas at Austin since it wasn't far from the new house. I decided to major in psychology and planned to use it to help women, like those on the compound, survive in the same ways my mama and I had learned to.

There were times I got a little down about the life I'd led before or how I'd spent twenty-eight years not knowing who my mama or daddy were. But not a day passed without Rip telling me how proud he was of me or how much he loved me. I heard him telling my mama how proud he was of her too, and that just made me love him more.

"You're deep in thought, darlin'," he said, coming up and putting his arms around me as I looked out at the sunlight on the water. "What's on your mind?"

"Just thinking about my life's dreams."

"Yeah? Have you come up with more you want to do?"

"Actually, I was thinking about how many have already come true."

"Like?"

"Well, I learned to ride a horse and drive a car. I have a phone that turns on lights in the house and even gets the coffee pot started in the morning. I know who my mama is, and I get to spend time with her every single day."

When I turned in his arms and rested my head on his chest, Rip leaned down and kissed the side of my face. "That was one too," I told him.

"What was?"

"I dreamed I'd find a man to love who'd love me back enough to snuggle me in his arms and kiss me the way you just did."

"I want to make every dream you've ever had come true, Pearl. There isn't anyone I know who deserves it more than you."

I shook my head. "I know someone who does."

He put his finger on my chin so I'd look up at him. "Who? Your mama?"

"My husband."

Keep reading for a sneak peek

at the first book in the

Unstoppables Series—

FURIED!

1

Fury

There was nothing like the burn of a neat shot of bourbon as the smooth liquid slid down my throat. I considered it a reminder of how pleasure could follow pain. As the warmth settled in my tummy then coursed through my veins, I looked over at the man who'd been my friend with benefits as he danced with the new woman in his life.

In all the years I'd known him, Rip never once looked at me the way he looked at Pearl. It hurt, but it was my pride that was wounded, not my heart. I'd known all along, in the same way he did, that we weren't "the one" for each other.

Rip had found his "it" girl, and I was happy for him in the same way he'd be happy for me if I ever found the man I was meant to spend my life with.

Now, though, sitting at the bar and wishing I was dancing like they were, sucked. Big time. Sure, there were a few men here tonight I could ask to two-step me around the crowded dance floor, and I'd certainly never been accused of being shy, but my heart wasn't in it.

Instead, I signaled Rebel, the bartender closest to me, for another shot.

"How ya doin' tonight, Fury?" she asked as she filled my empty glass with two fingers of the smoky dark-amber liquor I'd grown to love.

"You want the truth or a line?"

She smiled. "Always the truth, my friend."

"I'm feeling a little like the odd man out, as they say."

"I get that, this bein' a private party and all. No strangers here tonight; just the same ol', same ol'. Not that I care." Rebel was happily married to a man I'd run a mission or two with back when I was a CIA operative. I'd left that life, though, to pursue another form of the law as an attorney.

Edge and Rebel, like Rip and Pearl, were meant to be. Soul mates. Their suns rose and set for each other.

I downed the shots and was about to call it a night when I remembered I got here on my own and was in no shape to drive myself the thirty miles back to my house in the city. Getting a car service here in the hills outside Austin, Texas, would be impossible on any given night, but more so on a Sunday.

"Fuck," I muttered to myself since Rebel had walked away.

"Would you like to dance?" I heard a sultry Spanish-accented voice say from my right at the same time I felt a body brush up against mine. I slowly turned my head to see if the man looked as good as he sounded and was pleasantly surprised to discover he exceeded my hopes.

"Who are you?" I asked, surprised that there was anyone here tonight I didn't know, given, as Rebel had said, it was a private party.

"Leandro Barello III, but my friends call me Tres."

I looked down the length of him. Good Lord, the man was hotter than a ghost pepper. "How'd you sneak an invite to this shindig, Tres?"

"I'm actually working. I'm head bouncer here at the Long Branch."

"Yeah? Your bosses won't mind if you abandon your duties?"

"They encourage it. Maeve will tell you if you don't dance at least once a night, especially when you're working, you don't belong here."

Maeve, the wife of the attorney whose firm I joined a few months ago, was on the floor, dancing with her husband, Hammer. They'd purchased the bar around the same time the previous owner retired from "the scene," as he'd told everyone.

I knew the real reason, though; the man had stage-four cancer and didn't want to spend every night working the kind of hours a place like this required. Maeve and Hammer had been smart to hire a crew capable of running the Branch for them if they needed or wanted time away from it.

A chill coursed through me when Tres trailed his finger from my wrist up to my elbow, and I met his gaze.

"Dance with me, *niña hermosa.*"

Between his accent and his classically handsome looks, how could I say no?

When I woke the next morning, my mouth felt as though it had been stuffed with cotton balls. My head throbbed, and I was bare-ass naked—not the way I usually slept. And I wasn't alone. Tres-the-bouncer was in my bed, head propped on his bent arm, staring at me.

Rather than speak, he leaned forward and swirled my nipple with the tip of his tongue. While I didn't remember much of last night, memories of the pleasure his mouth brought me awakened my every nerve ending.

About the Author

USA Today and Amazon Top 15 Bestselling Author Heather Slade writes shamelessly sexy, edge-of-your seat romantic suspense.

She gave herself the gift of writing a book for her own birthday one year. Forty-plus books later (and counting), she's having the time of her life.

The women Slade writes are self-confident, strong, with wills of their own, and hearts as big as the Colorado sky. The men are sublimely sexy, seductive alphas who rise to the challenge of capturing the sweet soul of a woman whose heart they'll hold in the palm of their hand forever. Add in a couple of neck-snapping twists and turns, a page-turning mystery, and a swoon-worthy HEA, and you'll be holding one of her books in your hands.

She loves to hear from my readers. You can contact her at heather@heatherslade.com

To keep up with her latest news and releases, please visit her website at www.heatherslade.com to sign up for her newsletter.

MORE FROM AUTHOR HEATHER SLADE

BUTLER RANCH

Kade's Worth

Brodie's Promise

Maddox's Truce

Naughton's Secret

Mercer's Vow

Kade's Return

Butler Ranch Christmas

WICKED WINEMAKERS
FIRST LABEL

Brix's Bid

Ridge's Release

Press' Passion

Zin's Sins

Tryst's Temptation

WICKED WINEMAKERS
SECOND LABEL

Beau's Beloved

Coming Soon:

Cru's Crush

Bones' Bliss

Snapper's Seduction

Kick's Kiss

ROARING FORK RANCH

Coming Soon:

Roaring Fork Wrangler

Roaring Fork Roughstock

Roaring Fork Rockstar

Roaring Fork Rooker

Roaring Fork Bridger

THE ROYAL AGENTS
OF MI6

Make Me Shiver

Drive Me Wilder

Feel My Pinch

Chase My Shadow

Find My Angel

K19 SECURITY
SOLUTIONS TEAM ONE

Razor's Edge

Gunner's Redemption

Mistletoe's Magic

Mantis' Desire

Dutch's Salvation

K19 SECURITY
SOLUTIONS TEAM TWO

Striker's Choice

Monk's Fire

Halo's Oath

Tackle's Honor

Onyx's Awakening

K19 SHADOW OPERATIONS
TEAM ONE

Code Name: Ranger

Code Name: Diesel

Code Name: Wasp

Code Name: Cowboy

Code Name: Mayhem

K19 ALLIED INTELLIGENCE
TEAM ONE

Code Name: Ares

Code Name: Cayman

Code Name: Poseidon

Code Name: Zeppelin

Code Name: Magnet

K19 ALLIED INTELLIGENCE
TEAM TWO

Coming Soon:

Code Name: Puck

Code Name: Michelangelo

Code Name: Typhon

Code Name: Hornet

Code Name: Reaper

PROTECTORS
UNDERCOVER

Undercover Agent

Undercover Emissary

Coming Soon:

Undercover Savior

Undercover Infidel

Undercover Assassin

THE INVINCIBLES
TEAM ONE

Decked

Edged

Grinded

Riled

Smoked

THE INVINCIBLES
TEAM TWO

Bucked

Irished

Sained

Hammered

Ripped

THE UNSTOPPABLES
TEAM ONE

Furied

Merried

COWBOYS OF
CRESTED BUTTE

A Cowboy Falls

A Cowboy's Dance

A Cowboy's Kiss

A Cowboy Stays

A Cowboy Wins